For me Ma and Da.

blood red
TURNS DOLLAR GREEN
VOL. 2

THUNDERHEAD
PRESS

Edited by Úna Ryan.
Robbie Shorley.

ACKNOWLEDGMENTS

To Mick Foley, thank you for taking the time and the effort to help a complete stranger. I hope to be able to return the favor someday.

CHAPTER ONE

October 9th 1972.

Three days after Annie's murder.

New York.

Danno wanted to immediately follow his wife. When he heard. When he identified her. When he had to leave her there. When he arrived home alone. When he lay in their bed. And when he realized that he had nothing else that he wanted to live for.

He wanted to follow his wife. But he couldn't.

Not until he made right her death.

And if everyone in the business had to lose so he could do that – then so be it.

The car Danno was being taxied in bounced at odds with the weather-worn track underneath it. The heavy, wet branches rubbed and slapped the metal of the car until it eased through the tight woodland passage and could see the clearing. It was a quiet, flatland where a circle of parked cars shone their collective lights to form a midnight meeting place.

Apart from the invited, there was no one around for miles. There were only more empty forests and more darkness.

Upstate New York was a perfect place for Danno to start on his promise.

Ricky Plick's concerned eyes checked on his boss through the rearview mirror. He had been to Texas and back with his boss, on the most heartbreaking of trips. He kept looking back to see if Danno would give him the nod to turn the car around and get out of there.

But Danno didn't nod.

Ricky pulled into their assigned spot and added his headlights to the field's center stage. The rain walloped unevenly off the window in splashes.

"Let's get out of here boss," Ricky said calmly. "We can take our time to rethink this."

Ricky knew that Danno was a cerebral man. A man hardwired for strategy over rash decisions. It was that very same philosophy that kept Danno at the top of their business for the last few years.

"I'm not going anywhere," Danno simply replied as he watched Proctor King get dragged from one of the cars into the illuminated circle.

Proctor King was the boss over the Florida territory. Both he and Danno had a long, public, bitter dispute that escalated into a dangerous realm. A realm that brought threats to their families. Their rivalry ended only three nights before – with Danno outmaneuvering Proctor and taking over his Florida territory.

On finding out his territory was gone, Proctor warned Danno that he would get retribution. That same night, Danno's wife was murdered in a small Texan hotel room.

"Proctor was with us when ... it happened," Ricky reminded Danno.

The shine of the direct headlights and the torrent of rain made it hard for Proctor to see who summoned him. Having heard what happened to Annie Garland, he hoped it wasn't who he thought it was.

"Does he seem scared to you?" Danno asked Ricky as Proctor was forced to kneel down in the middle of the lights.

Ricky took a second before answering. "You don't need to do this."

"You can leave anytime you want," Danno replied.

Ricky had watched Danno enter into the cut-throat wrestling business late in his life. He saw for himself how Danno would be ignored and dismissed, but largely remain the same man – the same thoughtful and rational man. To others watching that was a sign of weakness but to reasonable men, like Ricky Plick, it was a sign of integrity. A quality that was about to leave him for good.

Danno opened his door and was quickly engulfed in the swirling wind and thick rain. The cars of the remaining bosses from the National Wrestling Council started their engines. This night's meeting put them all in a position that they would never ordinarily put themselves in – so one by one their cars left the water-soaked field and headed back to their hotels.

They showed their respect and unity by delivering Proctor. What Danno chose to do next, none of them wanted to see or be witness to. Although they all knew exactly what the intent was.

The hired hand, Mickey Jack Crisp, held an already stunned Proctor King in position on his knees.

"Danno," Proctor pleaded. "I had nothing to do with anything. You won fair and square. You got my territory."

Proctor looked down and saw a black plastic sheet being pulled into the grave it covered by the weight of the pooling rain.

The picture was starting to form into a reality.

"Jesus Christ, Danno. I didn't … I was with you. I didn't do anything," Proctor shouted.

"You don't have to do this," Ricky quietly pleaded as his haggard looking employer took his first steps into the remaining light.

"I didn't do it," Proctor said with his eyes firmly planted on Danno's.

"I told you that we were going to do this again someday," Danno said as he pulled a .38 Special from his pocket and put it to Proctor's right eye. "You threatened my family once before and I put a gun to your face, but I didn't act."

"Danno," he pleaded.

Proctor knew this wasn't like the other time. This time Danno was different. More sure of what he was going to do. Proctor knew for certain that if he didn't talk fast then his time above the soil was short.

He opened his mouth to speak but Danno pulled the trigger and pumped a single shot straight into his head. Proctor dropped forward and Danno watched the rain torpedo into the pool of blood running from his opened skull.

Danno could feel the air of shock rise from behind him. He could feel it rise from himself. The plan wasn't for Danno to take the shot. No one in the whole business thought he even had it in him – especially Ricky Plick.

Mickey Jack pushed Proctor's body onto the plastic with his foot. He wanted to get out of there as soon as possible. The money was great, but Proctor brought him into the wrestling business so he felt a little bad rolling him into the hole.

Ricky put his arm around Danno and steered him away.

"Now I want Curt Magee," Danno said as he shrugged Ricky off.

Ricky, very quietly and respectfully, pleaded with Danno to come with him. Danno hesitantly dropped the gun and walked back to his car.

"Not a word about this to anyone else. None of the other bosses can know what just happened," Ricky said to Mickey Jack.

Mickey Jack nodded.

"You took the shot, just like it was planned," Ricky said to Mickey Jack as he surveyed the area.

Ricky stooped and picked up Danno's discarded weapon and bundled it tightly in his jacket. He wasn't happy with how exposed Danno was now. Years of tightly wrapping him and keeping him squeaky clean – all gone.

Mickey walked over to his car, took out a gym bag and handed it to Ricky.

"Is the belt in there?" Ricky asked.

"Yep."

Ricky could tell by the weight of the bag that the World Heavyweight Title was inside.

Mickey Jack continued his work and began to fill in the hole.

"Can you stay in town for another couple of days? I might need you," Ricky asked as he walked away. "I'll know after Mrs. Garland's funeral tomorrow. Meet me at the same place at six."

Waiting in New York another day would be no problem to Mickey Jack. The wrestling guys always paid well and most of the time he had to do hardly anything to earn it.

From the car, Danno watched Proctor get buried. His wife was dead and he had just sent his first man to death. He needed to mourn but he couldn't yet, because he knew there would be more death to come.

CHAPTER TWO

The same night.

Nevada.

The driver was being driven.

Lenny Long sat in the passenger seat of the family car. After driving in shifts for nearly three days straight everyone was a little sharp. And the desert heat, even at night, really wasn't helping anything. They badly needed a change of scenery. They were in the same tired and bone dry car that escorted them all the way across from Florida.

The same car that escorted Lenny away from the wrestling business.

They only had time to drag all their worldly belongings into their tiny motel room before Bree got the call.

"Where is it?" Luke asked from the backseat. Both he and his toddler brother James Henry were truly sick of traveling and upheaval.

"Around the corner," Lenny lied.

"Is it?" Bree covertly mouthed.

Lenny shrugged. Vegas wasn't one of his towns. He had spent the last few years driving Danno Garland and his wife, Annie, wherever they needed to go. Just happened they never needed to go to Vegas.

"Do I make a right?" Bree asked as she anxiously navigated the sign-infested streets.

Lenny noticed the white tan lines of his wife's missing rings. He swore all the way from Florida that he'd make that better when he got himself settled and made some money.

"Right?" Bree asked again.

"I don't know about this," Lenny mumbled away from the children.

"About the right turn?" Bree asked.

"No, the job," Lenny replied.

Bree tapped the map on Lenny's lap to get him to focus. She had explained this to her husband a hundred times since she got the call the day before. "I'm just going to be dealing the cards. That's all."

"There's a reason they don't let women work in these places. Or didn't until now."

Bree gripped the steering wheel and talked herself out of another argument. Before they moved their whole lives across the country things hadn't been great between her and Lenny. His job with Danno meant that he was gone for weeks and sometimes months at a time. It nearly killed their marriage. This big shiny mess of a town was now their clean slate and Bree was doing her best not to dirty it.

"That's all they've asked you to do for now," Lenny said. "Deal cards, I mean."

"Just look for The Plaza."

Lenny snapped the map open in front of his face. "We're looking for Main Street."

Bree took a deep breath, "I know that." She tried to read all the hundreds of signs as they rolled by.

Every now and then Luke would crane his neck and 'whoa' at the pomp and cheap splendor of the buildings and their gimmicks. To Luke it looked like the town could have been designed by one of his seven-year-old friends. There were motel signs and restaurant signs and signs for shows and clubs and gas and coffee shops. Red signs, blue signs, round ones and small ones. Signs to tell you that there were signs ahead.

"Turn here," Lenny mumbled from behind the map.

"Here?"

"Yeah, here."

Bree began to think that maybe he was pulling them around in circles on purpose. She knew he didn't want to leave New York. She knew he didn't want to leave his job. She also knew he'd keep all that to himself.

"We should be coming up between First and Second street," Lenny said. The nose of their car guided them around the corner and onto a stacked street that presented itself as both beautiful and gaudy. Lights, bright colors, flags and banners. There was a giant cowboy and a huge star perched on the side of a casino. Down the end of the crammed, sparkling street The Union Plaza stood above them all. It was a light, tall and spurious design with a gaping foyer that sucked the road right in.

"Fuck, is that it?" Lenny asked.

"Says so right on top," Bree excitedly answered as she nodded Lenny's attention to the big red letters on the roof.

"And they're hiring ladies?" Lenny asked one last time.

Bree slowed down. "We could just go straight to my folks and stay there, Lenny."

"I wanna see Granpa," Luke said from the back.

Lenny shook his head. To him Las Vegas was the lesser of two evils. He may have been out of work, he may have been a near stranger to his kids – but Lenny was still the man of the Long house.

Or at least that's what he was trying to be.

He'd be damned if *his* wife would go to *her* folks looking for a place for *them* to stay. The motel was fine for now. And even though it made him nauseous – so was Bree's job.

Lenny put his hand on his wife's leg. She was beaming as the reflection of the hotel flicked across their windshield. She was happy. Her family were around her, she was getting to earn her own money, and she could work on things with her husband.

For the first time in a couple of years she was starting to think that maybe they could make it as a family.

Ricky didn't want to make the call. That feeling was familiar to him lately. He felt as though he spent most of his time doing things that were against his nature.

But business was business. And it was his job to protect the wrestling business at all costs.

He had parked outside a dingy bar about 10 miles from where they had left Proctor. It was dark and quiet and still pouring rain.

Ricky stood in the phone booth outside. He dialed and waited for a voice to pick up at the other end.

"Hello?" answered the voice.

"Gilbert?" Ricky asked.

"Who's this?"

"You know who it is. Where's Proctor?" Ricky asked.

"Ricky, I told you yesterday and the day before, I don't know. My mother doesn't know."

"Well, he's obviously jumped ship somewhere. If he couldn't take being Danno's champion then he should have been fucking man enough to say it. When you do see him, tell that weasel that I'm stripping him of the belt."

" I ... "

Ricky slammed the phone down and tried to manage his own disgust. He had already contacted the few wrestling media outlets that were left and spun the story that Proctor King wasn't man enough to accept a rematch with Babu.

Danno made the decision that Proctor had to go. Now Ricky had to clean up the fallout of that decision.

Danno went through the routine of getting undressed but to simply lie in an empty bed, after all those years of marriage, was strange and unusual. He wasn't glad to be home like he usually was. His house held nothing for him anymore.

Downstairs, Ricky was locking the doors and securing the house for the night.

"You okay up there?" Ricky shouted.

Danno didn't answer.

Ricky listened some more and took the silence to mean he was safe to proceed. He quietly walked into the hall and peered up the stairs to make sure Danno wasn't there. He then slid his hand into Danno's jacket and carefully took out a bunch of keys. Ricky removed one of the keys and placed the bunch back where he found them.

In his room Danno sat in silence as he was slowly being introduced to the restrictive frailty of being alone. All the years he worked and schemed to get the big house and the wall full of money meant absolutely nothing. Danno was left an old man, companionless.

In his head he harassed himself about the time he didn't talk to Annie for nearly a month because of something she said about his mother. He couldn't remember what. Or what about the time he frightened her after that dinner party? How he let her rot for years on those pills? The time he told her he couldn't have children?

He thought of Proctor's head pressed against his gun. The startling whack of noise as he pulled the trigger. It made him sick. All this made him sick. Seeing her laid out on the metal table. Knowing that the killer was still alive.

Danno got up and walked quickly to his bathroom where he stooped to vomit in his toilet bowl.

Just a few days ago, Danno was king. He managed to outmaneuver the other bosses to keep his New York territory and to add San Francisco and Florida to his budding empire. It all had to happen with precision. That's why he felt he had no choice but to agree with his wife when she suggested she go and negotiate for Texas.

Danno was the first boss in their business' history to move outside his own boundary lines and buy up other territories. That made him a huge threat to the other bosses. When was he coming for their patch? How long until he had the whole business to himself?

Danno thought about his celebration that night and everyone laughing and backslapping each other. He now knew that at the same time his wife was lying dead on the floor of a small, dingy hotel room in Texas.

It made him sick.

The thoughts of having to kill again made him sick. The thoughts of never seeing her again made him sick.

Danno sat on the floor of his bathroom and looked out to their bedroom. Or his room, now. It looked like old people lived there.

He remembered leaning into her cold ear and whispering, "I promise you I'll make this right before we meet again."

He couldn't lift his eyes from the bathroom floor. The only comfort he allowed himself was the fleeting thought that maybe Annie was waiting for him.

There was nothing else of meaning left in his life. And he was old and scared without her. The house was too big all of a sudden, and the noises outside were exhausting. Every couple of minutes he'd have to check a window to make sure there was nothing unusual coming his way.

Danno dragged himself off the bathroom floor and walked back into his room. He laid out his best suit on the end of the bed and checked the single bullet which lay in wait in the chamber of his chosen revolver.

It was a bullet, he knew, that had his name on it.

He slapped the cylinder closed and rested the gun beside his suit. Very soon he would return and dress himself in that suit and use that gun.

But not before he made good on his promise to his wife.

The next day. Four days after the murder.

New York.

The NYPD was down, riddled with systematic corruption and continually fending off accusations of crooked behavior. For many years the dysfunction was a private, dirty little secret, but now it was so well known that even Hollywood had begun to make movies about it.

It was an organization that was rotten from the top down. It was like an old boy's club that made false arrests, fabricated evidence, engaged in racketeering, beatings, bribery and even attempted murder.

The NYPD was a festering wound down the middle of a dying city.

Nestor Chapman tapped lightly on the one door in the world he hated entering. Even before the new guy showed up, Nestor hated that door.

"Come in," called the voice from inside.

Nestor turned the handle and walked sheepishly into the captain's office.

"Have a seat," Captain Miller said.

The captain reminded Nestor more of a doctor than a captain. He was near retirement, long and lean, and had a perfectly shiny bald head.

Nestor sat and tried to assess the situation. He had been in Miller's company a few times since Miller arrived from Brooklyn, but never on his own. He very much liked it that way.

"Did anyone ever tell Cooper that he types like a fucking retard?" the captain asked as he tried to make sense of a report on his desk.

Nestor smiled and nodded in league with his boss. The captain closed over his folder and focused solely on Nestor.

"Tell me what you know about Danno Garland," the captain said frankly.

Somewhere in his head, Nestor had been waiting for that question but when it came it still disarmed him a little.

"Well," he started. "Not much. He's a promoter here in the city. Across the north-east here. Wrestling. Or professional wrestling. Seems to have made some real money over the last few years judging by his... the way he lives now. I ... I ... he's ... low to the ground. Doesn't cause trouble. I don't know."

Miller watched Nestor's face very carefully. He leaned back in his creaky chair and thought for a second before following up.

"You've been following Troy Bartlett for a number of months," said the captain, making his words both a question and a statement.

Nestor nodded. He too leaned back and tried to make himself look less guilty of something.

"And this man, Troy Bartlett, is Danno Garland's lawyer?" the captain asked.

Nestor shrugged his shoulders and adjusted his body some more.

"And Danno's name never comes up when you're digging on this other guy?" Captain Miller asked.

"He does something for Garland but there's never been anything we could move in on. I'm interested in Bartlett for different matters. Missing monies. Shady practices. That kind of thing."

The captain again disconnected from the conversation to think. Nestor had heard how shrewd Miller was and how he played a tight game in terms of strategy. Such talents around this particular topic made Nestor anxious.

"Is there something?..." Nestor let his sentence trail off. He wanted to know what this was about but didn't want to ask directly. He knew that a high rank wasn't fishing around for nothing.

Captain Miller leaned into his desk and looked Nestor straight in the face. "I've got a US Senator who was stabbed in both legs a few blocks from here. I'm sure you've heard by now. It's everywhere. My goddamn wife has called me 10 times today to tell me it's on the radio and the TV."

"Yeah, I heard. Hell of a thing," Nestor answered, trying to sound sympathetic.

"Yeah well, the senator says he doesn't know what happened. He gets a lot of crazies, he says. Could have been anyone. He's calling for more money from the federal government for policing."

Nestor nodded accordingly. "This city is … everyone who goes out there is on their own," Nestor replied, sounding totally unaware of his responsibility.

"Well, we might have something to do with that. Don't you

think?" the captain asked.

Nestor realized how stupid his answer was. He wanted to get the conversation back on track. "What makes you think Garland had anything to do with it?"

The captain stood up and walked to the mesh-covered window. "When the news broke, I personally got a call from the head of the Athletic Commission. He comes down here to our boxing club. Maybe you've seen him around. Melvin Pritchard? Anyways, he says that the Senator, just before he was attacked, was scheduled to bring Garland before a committee on match fixing or some such nonsense."

Miller turned back from the window slowly and rested his hand against the wall.

"I didn't know that," Nestor lied.

"US Senators don't get stabbed on the street in the United States of America. Not even in this fucking city. I just need to know whether I should chase this wrestling guy or discount him and move on. 'Cause someone is gonna notice … "

The captain stopped himself.

And there it was, Nestor thought. The money shot. The reason he was called in at all. A high ranking politician with a national profile gets knifed on the street and someone is either getting squashed for mishandling it or highly rewarded for fixing it. There had been talk around the department of the First and Fourth precincts being amalgamated under one roof. No police house in the whole of New York had two captains.

Nestor thought that Miller was fixing to move up the chain.

"This police force can't afford another high profile fuck up," the captain said. "If they're going to make another movie about us … it's gotta be … we've … we're the good fucking guys you understand?"

Nestor nodded in agreement. Captain Miller looked at his detective and couldn't decide on him one way or the other.

"I've ordered some officers to go out and shake a few bushes. Make a few inquires into this Garland person."

Nestor nodded.

"Just so you know," the captain said.

"Okay," Nestor answered, not quite knowing what he should say.

"I've asked every cop in this building to bring me what they know about Danno Garland." The captain sat back down and lifted his pen, ready. "So you have nothing to tell me in this regard at this time?"

Nestor shook his head. "Not at this time," he said.

"But when you do … "

"But when I do … "

Nestor sat easy even though he felt like bursting out the door and running to his car. He knew he needed to stay ahead of what was coming.

Luckily he had already started.

Danno descended the large creaky stairs dressed in a black suit. He really tried to resist it but in the end he felt compelled to shout. "Hello?"

He wasn't sure whether he wanted somebody to reply or not. It was just something he did now. Now that he was there on his own.

He picked up his phone and dialed Lenny Long from his pocket phone book. The number just returned a disconnected tone. Danno tried again but got the same result.

He noticed a note lying on the floor just by his front door. He carefully walked towards it and checked the doorways of his house before he stooped.

He opened it, and it read:

There's a heatwave coming up from Florida. You better cover up.

He didn't recognize the handwriting. But the headed paper was something he had seen a thousand times before.

CHAPTER THREE

Ricky woke and gingerly put his right leg out of the bed first and tried to gauge the level of pain present, before coaxing his much worse left leg to follow suit. Both actions sent a stabbing sensation to the base of his neck, which in turn rang as a squeal of pain in his ears.

Most retired wrestlers woke up in the same way after years of taking bumps in the ring – cautiously. *Knowing* when you're going to be slammed, tossed and dropped doesn't lessen the pain of *being* slammed, tossed or dropped.

Pain or not, Ricky made sure not to make too much noise because he didn't want to wake Ginny who was still asleep beside him.

Ricky many times prayed that there was never an emergency at night because neither man would be able to get out of bed in time to survive. They both had long careers and were now paying the physical price.

Mornings were the worst.

He shuffled out of their bedroom and cracked various bones along the way. He softly closed the door between their bedroom and the kitchen. He fired up the radio and news came through the speakers:

" … Mr. Tenenbaum left the hospital and was driven to an unknown location. Eye witnesses recounted the Senator's struggle in simply entering the waiting vehicle because of the dressing on both his legs."

Ricky quickly flicked the off button. Hearing the report sent a chill through his body which further reaffirmed that that side of the business was something he wanted to stay many, many miles from.

Ricky was a wrestling man through and through. Had been all his life. He was Danno's number two – The Booker. He was responsible for making the matches and deciding the winners. It was his responsibility to make the card new and exciting every time he entered a different town.

Danno handled the office, contracts and business and Ricky handled everything once they were on the road.

He dearly wished that they could get back to that, but he wasn't sure Danno was thinking the same way. Or that he ever would again. He knew that Danno's actions were leaving the business too exposed, too open. Ricky was going to need to work smart and try to cover all the bases that Danno was missing.

There was still the business to run. A business which fed on politics and sleight-of-hand. And a card at Madison Square Garden.

Ginny stood at the sink of their small apartment. He wore a fresh white vest and his short hair was washed and slicked back with a comb. His stubbled face was half covered in soap while the other side was clean-shaven. Back in the day, Ginny used to shave with a blade, just like his father before him. Now he needed Ricky's help to get the right side of his face done.

Ever since his car got smashed off the highway, things had been tougher for Ginny. And Ricky.

"Don't leave the spot under my nose," Ginny said.

Ricky looked over his glasses and gently navigated his way around his partner's face.

Ginny pointed impatiently. "There. Under my nose. There."

Ricky swirled the razor around in the water and tapped it twice off the side of the sink.

"I heard you," Ricky said.

Every day was the same. Ginny liked to be fresh faced. He just couldn't trust his own hand to stay steady anymore.

Ricky placed the razor on Ginny's neck and Ginny tilted his head in sync.

"The bit," Ginny said pointing under his nose.

"I'm going to slit your throat if you don't stop bothering me," Ricky warned.

Ginny grabbed the small mirror and checked under his nose as Ricky continued.

"You know, it would be easier to do this if you just stayed still," Ricky said.

Ginny burst into tears. Ricky stopped what he was doing but otherwise didn't even acknowledge it. The first few times Ginny cried like that after he came out of the hospital, Ricky rallied around and begged Ginny to tell him what was wrong. Now, the tears just came and went. They were for nothing. They meant nothing. Neither man mentioned them anymore.

And as soon as they came, Ginny wiped his tears, and they were gone. Ricky continued his morning job.

"Under my nose," Ginny said rubbing his eyes with his forearm.

Ricky also ignored Ginny's orders. The head trauma left him repetitive, cognitively slower, more moody and emotional. He couldn't reach across his body and he suffered from debilitating headaches.

At the beginning Ricky wanted his old Ginny back. Now he just accepted the way he was. After all their years together, and remembering how close he came to losing him, Ricky was just happy to have him any way he could.

"Why is there a gun hidden under our bed?" Ginny asked with crystal clarity.

That's the way it went. Confusion to clarity. Neediness to independence. It changed hour to hour and minute to minute.

"You know what the city is like out there now," Ricky replied.

"It's wrapped up though. Like you're trying to hide it."

"No," Ricky lied. "I got it for us. Do you want to leave your life in the hands of the cops we got?"

The morning light highlighted all of Ginny's scarring. The back of his head. Across his right shoulder, down the triceps and around the forearm. He was already too beat up to continue wrestling before he got rammed off the highway.

"I want us out," Ginny said as he flung the hand towel onto his shoulder and rubbed the side of his face dry.

"Out of what?" Ricky asked, knowing perfectly well what Ginny was talking about.

The phone on the wall in the kitchen began to ring. Ricky hurried, like an old person hurries, to answer the call. "Hello?"

"We got to meet up," the voice on the line said plainly.

Ricky immediately recognized the voice. "Okay," he answered.

"At the end of the bridge tonight at 10."

"Can't. I've got to tape our TV shows. How about four?"

"Is Danno going to be there?" the voice asked.

"I doubt it," Ricky replied.

The caller hung up.

Nevada.

Lenny lay unconscious on the pink carpet of his motel room. James Henry silently watched his father intently from behind the prison bars of his crib.

"Do it," Lenny whispered without moving his lips.

"I don't want to," Luke answered anxiously from his standing position on the bed.

Lenny squinted an eye open. "You've laid me out son. Now finish me."

Luke didn't really like wrestling anymore but he missed playing with his father. "I ..."

"Big splash or elbow son, this is your big finish. Listen to that crowd chant your name and you pick your spot," Lenny said as he reprised his role of prone wrestler.

Luke awkwardly jumped/fell and landed with a double knee drop right across his father's face. An angry and wounded noise escaped from Lenny as he rolled into the fetal position and cradled his own head in pain. It was so intense that he was afraid to breathe.

Luke stood and walked backwards until he felt the multi-colored bed at the back of his legs. He watched his father eventually draw in narrow, short painful breaths. "Dad?"

Lenny rocked back and forth and moaned a little.

"I'm sorry," Luke said.

Lenny wanted to let his son know he was fine but it felt like his jaw, nose and skull were broken. "S'fine," is all he could release from his lungs.

Luke came closer and put a little hand on his father's shoulder. The baby in the cot threw his bottle and clapped and gurgled at nothing in particular.

"You have to protect the people you work with," Lenny said and tapped his little boy's hand.

Luke cuddled into his father's back and whispered into his ear, "I don't like wrestling anymore."

That was even more painful to Lenny. All he could do was lie there and retrain his sight around the room. Pea green seats. Check. Wood paneling. Check. Uneven wardrobe. Check. Stacks of cash underneath that same wardrobe.

What the fuck? Lenny thought to himself.

Luke nestled the top of his head into his father's neck and figured out a comfortable spot to snuggle.

"Bath time," Lenny said shrugging him off. "Take your brother."

"I don't want to …"

"Do it," Lenny ordered. "Fill up the tub and put your little brother in it."

"I don't know how. Mom does that," Luke argued.

"Get in there now and close the door."

Luke struggled to lift his little brother from the crib. He managed to drag his legs over the top bar and awkwardly walked into the bathroom and closed the door. Lenny pulled himself closer to the money.

He knew he had just found his wife's stash. The same one she told him she didn't have anymore. The same stash she took from a bag that Lenny had been hiding in their garage. She took it because she thought it was Lenny's. She thought it was theirs.

It wasn't.

The short journey fittingly took Lenny along Paradise Road. Bree was working the second day of her new job and he knew he could be there and back to the motel before she got off her shift. He didn't tell her where he was going - or more importantly - why he was going there because he made a promise.

A promise he was going to break.

The night before Lenny lay in his new, rock hard bed and watched his wife sleeping. He hadn't got to do that much over the previous four years. He was reminded why he loved her. And he hoped that she wasn't coming to the realization that she might have just settled for him.

He adored her and his boys.

But that didn't mean that he wasn't going to lie to them.

He pulled into the curb and stalked the little store on the other side of the busy Vegas street. "I'll be back in a second," he told his young sons as he cracked open his car door.

"Where are you going Daddy?" Luke asked from the backseat, trying to move his little brother from his lap.

He too could see clearly across the road and in his seven short years he had never had to wait in the car while his mother went into a store.

"I'll be a second. You wait here and look out for your little brother."

James Henry immediately put out his arms for his father to pick him up. He was a lazy child who didn't speak much for a two year old. He just kinda sat there – cute, with clear skin and a blonde, round, doughy head.

"He wants to go with you," Luke said, volunteering himself as translator.

"Just tell him I'll be a second. Can you do that?" Lenny replied, taking him up on his offer.

"He's going to cry, Dad."

"No, he's not." Lenny closed his door and wiped the sweat of the desert from his brow.

James Henry immediately began to bawl. Lenny couldn't believe his luck. A crying child instantly stressed him out. He thought about pulling Bree out of her job and marching her home.

What kind of man looks after the kids while the wife works?

He looked at the two little distressed faces looking out from the dirty back window. "I just wanted to go to the store – right there – to get you both some candy," he shouted and mimed in an attempt to cross the road guilt free.

It wasn't going to work. James Henry's bottom lip grew bigger with sorrow.

How does Bree calm them down?

Lenny remembered her saying something to him about cassettes one night after he came off the road.

"Do something Dad," an equally flustered older brother said from the backseat.

Lenny got back in the car and rummaged in the glove compartment. He pulled out a few battered eight-tracks and turned on the ignition. He slipped a tape into the player and soon a sweet a capella children's song came on. Lenny watched his youngest son's face turn from despair to curiosity.

"Mom," Luke joyfully pronounced.

Lenny panicked a little before he realized his boy was talking about the song. The little one was right – it was Bree. She was singing a song in that beautiful voice that Lenny hadn't heard in a lot of years.

"I will get you something nice," he mouthed to the older one as he put his finger to his lips and slipped out of the car.

Luke watched as his father dodged the heavy traffic to get to the store. He desperately tried to see further but couldn't with his brother on his lap. He rolled down the window and the cars outside sped past inches from his face.

The waiting was agony. Luke pushed James Henry off his legs and rose to his knees and peeked slightly out the window. Lenny was still nowhere to be seen.

He peeked again.

Maybe he's buying me a new Etch-a-Sketch like Dory Pike has back home?

James Henry was 'singing' along with his mother and happily waving his See n' Say around.

Luke thought his brother would be fine there alone if he went and had a closer look. He carefully opened his own door and dropped his small foot onto the sticky Vegas road. His opened door was way too tall for him to see over so he couldn't judge the oncoming traffic. He stooped for a better view and watched the cars hurtling towards him.

On the back seat, James Henry was also crawling towards the door. The sounds, and adventure his big brother was taking, were even more curious than the song.

"Stay there, James Henry," Luke demanded, to no avail. "Do you hear me? Only I'm big enough," he said.

The baby propped himself up in a seated position in front of Luke and playfully threw his toy into the road. Luke turned and absentmindedly followed the course of the toy.

"Luke," Lenny shouted as he stuffed a brown paper bag into his shirt from the other side of the road.

Luke froze with fear a foot into the road.

"Go back to the car," Lenny shouted.

He knew by his son's face that he was shocked and confused. Lenny could also see a red Pontiac speeding closer to his child.

He manically tried to jostle with the traffic on his side to make it to his boy.

"Luke, get back to the car now," Lenny ordered.

Luke didn't move. He couldn't.

"Run."

The little boy just stood in place, totally helpless.

"Turn around Luke," Lenny screamed.

Luke turned to face the oncoming car. Lenny launched himself through the small, dangerous gaps in the traffic and snatched his son up into his arms, just as the red Pontiac sped past.

"I'm sorry Daddy. I wanted to see where you went to," Luke said as he cried with fright on his father's shoulder.

"It's okay, little man," Lenny said as he moved his baby back safely into the seat. Luke was vined around his body as Lenny got in himself. "It's okay."

Lenny, Luke and James Henry sat in the back of the Long family car listening to Bree sing them a lullaby as the craziness of Las Vegas rumbled outside their windows.

Lenny began the stomach churning audit of events, detailing the very narrow miss.

"What have you got in the bag, Daddy?" Luke asked through his floods of tears.

"Nothing son," Lenny lied.

CHAPTER FOUR

New York.

The floor to ceiling glass panel windows were making everyone nervous outside the church. The wrestlers on top of the card – those that could afford it – stayed in their blacked-out limos for fear of being seen socializing with their 'sworn enemies.' The lower card wrestlers dispersed themselves around the grounds until the sermon began. There didn't seem to be anyone from the public around – but that's not to say any of the wrestlers would be forgiven by their promoters for 'breaking character' either.

Ricky walked the pathway that was cut through the manicured gardens of the church grounds. The tree branches overhead leaned across each other to form a woven guard of honor. He knew it was going to be a long day. He liked Annie and missed her terribly too. Not that anyone was going to be thinking of him and his problems.

In the absence of Danno, Ricky was unofficially appointed the Wrestler's Wailing Wall.

All disputes, matches, wrestling cards and wrestler problems just fell to him by proxy. But Ricky had his own problems. All he was focused on was Ginny, alone and slightly confused looking, by the church door. Ricky wanted to put his arms around him and help him tuck in his ruffled shirt. He wanted to put his arms around him and protect what he had become – a joke to the younger wrestlers who took every single opportunity to disrespect and laugh at him when his back was turned.

Ricky could see it, but he couldn't do anything to stop it. Because, like everything in the wrestling business, there was a facade that must be kept intact at all times. None of The Boys worked with fags. None of The Boys would shower with them or be seen with them. And The Boys certainly wouldn't take orders from one.

So Ricky guiltily walked past his partner's smile and outstretched right hand and marched straight into the church. For both their sakes.

On his way down the hard stone aisle he was grabbed gently by a well-pressed Texan. "The Garden is flat, Ricky," Wild Ted Berry said in a hushed tone.

Ricky nodded in acknowledgement. His silence didn't impress Bill one bit. "I'm telling you that The Garden is flat and all you can do is nod?"

Ricky nodded again and continued towards the top pew.

They were to tour around and finish their loop once a month at The Garden. That was the New York company's stronghold. The building where they always gave a little more. A title match, a TV taping, a cage match – something extra. Something you don't see at every card.

Others expected a sold-out house but Ricky was more realistic. The last time they ran a card in New York was only a couple of weeks before, and they didn't deliver their main event. It was the most hyped and anticipated main event in their history. The New York crowd rioted and tore up Shea Stadium where they had paid to see it. Not enough time had passed for them to forget.

That's why the house was flat.

"Just a note of condolence for the boss," The Folsom Nightmare said before Ricky could build up a head of steam.

Ricky took the card. "I'll make sure he gets it."

"Terrible day."

Ricky again nodded and tried to move on.

"Doc says I'm good to go," Folsom said without real conviction. "My Achilles is healed all back up. Healed, get it?"

Ricky looked along the row and could see one of Folsom's many young sons trying valiantly to hide his father's crutch under the pew. Wrestlers who didn't wrestle didn't get paid and there were a lot of young faces looking in Ricky's direction.

"Folsom... " Ricky began.

Folsom leaned in closer to talk about business. "I could start back in Battle Royals or something. The Boys will look out for me, Ricky. I could come over the top and take a bump on my back or something. I don't need to put pressure on my foot straight away."

Ricky could see a proud father pleading with him in front of his family.

"We'll give it some more time," Ricky said as he lay a useless hand on Folsom's shoulder. "You'll be back soon."

Folsom forced a smile.

"You'd think Proctor King would have at least shown to pay his respects," Ricky said as he left.

He walked away with a heavy heart knowing that The Folsom Nightmare, hurt in the ring, would never wrestle again.

He also knew that Proctor not being there would spread like wildfire.

Midgets, beauty queens, tattooed faces, gold sunglasses, new black suits, hugely obese twins, a bald old woman, toothless mountain men, islanders, a one-legged man and a giant.

Christ Church was stuffed with representatives from all over the wrestling world. All the other bosses from the National Wrestling Council were there. Even though their Annual General Meeting was officially off, promoters from Japan, Europe and Africa still arrived. They all wanted to make sure that Danno saw them sad. If they could only swing one tour with Danno's huge champion they could roll in the money. So they did what any self-respecting promoter would do – they out-cried each other.

"Where's the boss?" Ricky asked the huddled crowd at the top pew. Nobody knew.

Across the aisle, the chairman of the National Wrestling Council, Joe Lapine, wondered where Danno was too. Beside him stood the boss of the Carolinas, Tanner Blackwell.

"Danno killed his own champion," Tanner said to Joe.

"I tried for days to talk him out of it," Joe replied. "He was blind with rage."

None of the bosses ever cry when a world title gets taken from someone. This increases the chances significantly that they are next in line to receive it.

"I heard he did it himself?" Tanner said to Joe.

Joe leaned in and whispered, "What?"

"Last night. Danno did the job himself."

Joe shook his head disbelievingly. "No way."

Tanner smiled.

Hiring someone from outside to kill is one thing. The guy with the whole business in his hands doing the killing was something completely different.

"Not in a million years," Joe said.

Joe, like everyone else, didn't think Danno Garland had it in him to kill. But Tanner knew. He paid to find out.

The priest shuffled from the sacristy door and his jowly face hung down like a melted candle. His entrance cued the gathering to daydream about being champion, having the champion or who held them back from being champion.

For those in the wrestling business, those three permutations of the one possession gnawed and prodded at them and demanded most of their time.

With that heavyweight title came a lot of power and a lot of money. There wasn't a single person in attendance who didn't want both.

Ricky looked at Annie's casket and couldn't help but imagine what her last seconds were like. The cops wouldn't tell Danno much more than where she was found and how she was killed. They hadn't got to the *who* part yet. They said some prints were found and a man was seen walking towards her room.

"Please rise," the priest said from the altar.

Danno had been such an infrequent visitor that the priest never even noticed that the husband of the deceased wasn't even in attendance.

Ricky noticed though.

Outside, Danno stood with his back to the church wall and his face in the sun. He couldn't walk through the doors. His legs just wouldn't do it. He couldn't be close to her again until he fulfilled his promise.

"He's started," Ricky said from the large arched doorway in his most gentle voice.

"Did you find Curt Magee yet?" Danno said without looking away from the sky.

Ricky was uncomfortable with just how loose Danno was with his words in public. "I'm trying to keep things moving with the business. All the other bosses are in town and we have The Garden coming up."

Danno turned directly to his long time confidante. "Fuck the business, Ricky. You find the man who killed my wife. You track him down and you fucking hold him till I get there. Do you hear me?"

Through the window Ricky could see everyone straining to look at them outside. Even the priest was distracted.

"Do you hear me?" Danno asked again, suddenly becoming overwhelmed. He stopped himself crying. "How can I go in there to her? How can I stand in the same room as that poor woman when I haven't made it right?"

"I'm sorry about what happened. My heart is broken for you but …"

"But what?"

Ricky walked a little closer and spoke a little softer. "Boss, you need to let yourself grieve or mourn or whatever it is people do at times like this."

Up close and on their own, Ricky could see just how broken Danno was. He was missing.

"I just want him to feel like I do," Danno said.

"I know."

"No, you don't. I want the bastard to feel exactly like I did when I heard. Like I did when I had to see her laid out like that. I want his family to feel that loss. Like I am."

Danno moved to leave. "And I will. If it's the last thing I do on this earth. I will make good on my promise. And I'll transfer this pain I have onto them."

Ricky struggled to verbalize his reluctance to follow his boss. Such words were unfamiliar to him but Ricky was simply a retired wrestler – a man who loved the wrestling business. He wasn't a detective or hitman and, unlike a lot of the people at the ceremony, he had no desire to be.

Ricky followed him. "Where are you going?"

"If I have to ask for their help instead of yours then I will," Danno said about the other bosses. "I want Curt Magee found or I'm going to go like a tornado across all the territories until I find him."

Danno walked for the large gates as Ricky stopped in his tracks.

"Cause someone out there knows where he is," Danno shouted back.

Ricky tried to figure out how to cool all this down. He knew that Danno accusing the other bosses of hiding a murderer wasn't going to end up good. Bosses can't just take each other out whenever they feel like it. That makes everyone at the top nervous.

In the wrestling business funerals only grant you pity for a day. Then it's all about the money again.

A weak and unfocused Danno was a gift to everyone who wanted what he had. And Ricky knew that everyone in that church was using the opportunity to gauge just how wounded Danno was.

Nevada.

Lenny felt stupid and childish and secretive. And excited. He simply didn't want word getting back to his wife that he was back looking at this sort of thing again.

So a purple, tiled public restroom it had to be.

He sat in the stall and silently pulled out the brown bag from inside his shirt. Luke sat on the floor directly outside his father's stall with a mouth full of candy and his little brother on his lap, sucking on a popsicle. Their faces were a pleasurable, sugary mess and their fingers were too sticky to part.

Luke dropped one of his sweets on the restroom floor. He waited for his father's instruction to leave it where it fell. It never came, so he wiped the escaped sweet and popped it in his mouth.

"You nearly finished in there, Dad?" Luke asked with his mouth full.

Lenny pulled a magazine from his paper bag and delicately opened it. He missed those glossy pages. The smell of a new publication.

USA WRESTLING CHRONICLES.

"Dad?" Luke again asked. "Are you nearly finished in there?"

A stranger entered and tried to figure out what two little boys where doing sitting on the floor of a public restroom.

The seven-year-old's arm was still in one sleeve of his jacket but the other empty sleeve was running underneath the stall where Lenny was standing on it. Like holding a dog on a leash.

"Nearly finished, son," Lenny answered.

The bemused stranger went about his business.

Lenny couldn't wait any longer to see if his debut as a referee made the magazines. Growing up in Long Island, Lenny used to buy stacks of those same magazines to catch up on all the matches and new champions in the wrestling world. He religiously tore out the center poster and replaced the image on his wall, based on who was new and cool. One man never got replaced on the Long wall though – The Sugarstick Shane Montrose. Lenny considered this his reconnaissance. After all, he'd have to know what was happening in the wrestling world if he was to go back. It was just a pity that wrestling magazines were always weeks behind.

In the middle of Las Vegas, with his kids on the floor and his wife dealing cards, Lenny Long was the happiest man in the world. Because of wrestling.

It would soon make him feel a whole lot different.

New York.

The old back bar room was dark and smoky. Even the process of mourning had to be kept away from the public. Every major boss and their top wrestling stars were dotted along the chipped tables and cozy booths.

When someone of note in the wrestling business dies, it's a good networking opportunity. When someone belonging to a boss dies — you better be there or your name gets blackened. But when the wife of a boss gets killed, and the killer is still out there, you *better be* there or theories start to form and questions begin to get asked.

And so, Annie Garland's wake was standing room only.

The back room of a nightclub wasn't where Annie Garland should have been remembered — but rules are rules. Protect the business at all times.

Even when business is the last thing on your mind.

Danno sat alone, and in thought, at the top of the room. Everyone was giving him space and time. He wasn't eating, he wasn't drinking. And he wasn't talking. Most of the other 'mourners' were trying to figure out how long is respectful enough to stay sober.

They were all together, on a day off, in a bar. That never happened. And the temptation to capitalize on that perfect storm of circumstance was excruciating.

Even with the bar signs covered over and the tables draped in flowers — it was still a shit-hole and Danno knew it.

A bar like this would have been the last place a woman like his wife would go if she was alive.

Outside, The Sugarstick Shane Montrose, hurried and late, marched down the dark alleyway towards the wake.

As always, he was dressed in style. His suit was beige pinstripe with matching bellbottoms and a single breast pocket. Gold button. His shirt was blue and his tie was red silk with a paisley design. Shane Montrose was one of the biggest wrestlers of all time. Over his many years in the business he saw and did it all — nearly. And that life was evident for all to see on his handsome, but aging, overly-tanned face.

He was a man in his mid fifties who looked a whole lot older.

He was also a mess of drink and cocaine. He could carry neither with style or dignity. Anytime he got drunk or stoned he was a fucking lunatic. Which was often. On both counts.

But in wrestling he was a draw. He was someone the people were willing to pay to see no matter what territory he was in. In his business he had done it all. Except be champion. Only the heavyweight championship of the world eluded him.

For now, he thought.

He nervously walked to the designated back door and was immediately recognized by a star struck rookie wrestler who got the job of doorman. Shane tipped him with a hundred. He tipped everyone, all the time.

He slowly took the steep stairs and waited to reclaim his breath when he reached the top. He fixed his hair and made sure all his jewelry was facing the right way. The sounds inside were muted but large. He knew it was a full room of scumbags and whores doing their best not to enjoy themselves too much in front of the boss who had the champion.

It was a long time since Shane Montrose was nervous.

But this time he had good reason to be.

In the dingy restroom Danno robotically washed his hands. Most everything he was doing now was from preprogramming. Autopilot.

The restroom door opened and Joe Lapine, the Chairman of the NWC entered. Danno watched him in the mirror and he stood with the stall door open and took a piss.

"How are you holding up, Danno?" Joe asked.

Danno didn't know how to answer such a question. So he didn't.

"I don't even know what to say to you," Joe said as he finished up. "It's a tragedy." He flushed and took up a spot washing in the sink next to Danno.

Danno realized he had washed his hands twenty times over and the cuffs of his shirt were soaking wet.

"I wanted to stay with you last night," Joe said as he checked to make sure the stalls were empty. "Because no man should go through that alone."

Danno never even looked up.

Joe caught Danno's eye in the mirror.

"I appreciate you giving me the Chair when you could have taken it for yourself. So I'm glad we could set that up for you," Joe said, reminding Danno that he brought Proctor, and Mickey Jack to kill him, the night before.

Danno rubbed his hands on the worn-out towel that was barely clinging to the wall.

"Someone said you … " Joe stopped and looked around again. " … did the deed?"

Joe could clearly see that Danno didn't want to talk about it so he changed the subject. "Now, we all just want to help you move on, Danno."

"Move on?" Danno asked, his voice raspy from lack of use.

"Move on," Joe reiterated. "To get back to business."

Danno cleared his throat so there would be no misunderstanding in what he was about to say. "You think I'm finished looking for him, Joe?"

"We hope that you are. All of us. It's best for business."

Danno dried his hands, reached for the door and walked back into the packed room.

Joe said, "The National Wrestling Council stands with … "

Danno was gone and Joe didn't even bother to finish his sentence.

January 10th 1969.

Three years before the murder.

Oregon.

The National Wrestling Council was a collection of men who owned the largest wrestling territories in the Americas. It was set up to prevent other wrestling outfits from starting up and eating into their pie in such areas.

For many years, they patrolled and promoted successfully without too much of a challenge. People knew better than to try.

Merv Schiller sat as president of the National Wrestling Council since its inception in the mid-forties. Over the years he had positioned himself so as to own the table that everyone else dined at.

They met frequently, as needed, to discuss business matters, wrestler trades and decide who was going to be Heavyweight Champion of the World.

The owner who got the champion got rich. The money goes where the champ goes – and the power goes where the money goes. So the owner who got the champion essentially ran the syndicate by proxy.

All eyes were now on the main item of the agenda. Danno's stomach had been upset just thinking about it.

Merv rechecked his notes as he rolled his fat cigar around his brown fingers. "No change," he announced from behind his huge glasses. "That's the verdict."

The small, smoky, back room acted animated like the outcome was a shock. Danno did all he could to hide his devastation.

"There's no need," Merv continued above the mostly feigned

disquiet. "Sal Pellington is a good champ for us and a good draw along the west coast. So, no change."

Merv, it just so happened, owned the west coast territory, had control of Sal Pellington and was chairman of the NWC.

"What about the rest of us, Merv?" asked an aggressive Curt Magee from Texas. "How are we supposed to eat?"

"With your fucking mouth," the slight, old chairman spat back.

Curt looked around the room for anyone as shocked as him. "Did you say 'with your fucking mouth' or 'watch your fucking mouth'?"

"Both." Merv wound up and knocked out his most worn line, "None of you are tied to this council."

Danno knew he had been screwed over again. He brought Missus Garland and put her up in the Governor Hotel, such was his confidence this time. She even wore them under-britches that very seldom see anything but the bottom drawer.

Annie Garland sat in the foyer half reading from her book and half watching the door. She looked out for any sign of Danno – although she knew he'd be hours yet before he returned from his big meeting. Her heart was full with excitement. And guilt. But she felt she couldn't help it. For days she had tossed the word 'compelled' around in her head. That's all she could think to call her wants. She felt, and was, compelled.

"You ready?" whispered a moving voice behind her.

Annie took one last look at the giant, glass front door and satisfied herself that the coast was clear. She quickly followed Shane Montrose into the waiting elevator.

Back at the meeting, Danno felt stupid for even believing that he had a deal. Eight months previously he had flown all the bosses in to see his giant seven foot prospect beat Ricky Plick in a hell of a main event in the New Jersey Armory. He knew it was a small crowd, but a great match and a true attraction wrestler gave Danno the nod over the other potential champions in line.

It was all sealed by a crystal clink in his office backstage. Everyone was going to get rich off this huge kid. The members of the NWC were happy and unanimous that the belt be dropped to the giant after their next official meeting in Portland, Oregon.

This meeting.

Shane hurriedly opened the door to his room and scooped Annie off her feet. His wrestling dates had kept them both apart for the best part of a year. She adored him, missed him. She loved him. She wondered if he felt the same. He must have. He made it his business to get to Oregon. To her.

He was a mercenary his whole career. He traveled where the best money was and he never had any problems letting the bosses know that. He was a rare thing in the wrestling business in that he got over with the audience no matter how many times a promoter tried to make an example out of him by making him lose. He once lost four straight title matches in the same building and he still managed to sell it out the next week.

And he did it all with a microphone.

He knew how to make people feel the way he wanted them to feel. He knew how to garner sympathy and rally soldiers of support in the stands. He could do what all truly great wrestlers could – he could manipulate people. And the bosses loved that. Not that they'd ever let the wrestlers know that.

Annie knew it was no coincidence that he was here at the same time the NWC was meeting here too. Still, she let herself be fooled. He was here for her.

"Okay, let's move on to any other business," Merv said as he pushed his glasses onto his forehead and shuffled some papers.

Danno cleared his throat and the meeting left a respectful silence for his potential input. He stood up.

"We had a deal, Merv." Danno looked around the room to see which of the other owners had knifed him in the back. "But more than that, I have someone who we know people are going to pay to see. I have someone who you all watched work a few months ago; someone who could make us all a lot of money. Now I've kept him under wraps for months, waiting for the nod today. I was going to explode this kid onto the scene and get the world talking."

"He was green as goose shit and we need to move on to other business, Danno," Merv interrupted.

"But I have a question," Danno fired back.

"Make it quick," Merv said.

Fuck it. Danno had nothing to gain anymore by being polite anyway. "Yeah, just one point. Would you still be reneging on our deal if the giant jumped to your company like you quietly asked him to do several times last week?"

The occupants of the room turned squarely to Merv to hear his response. Danno simply asked what everyone else was thinking.

"In my life I've never been so insulted and … and … what's the word … ?"

Danno instinctively finished his sentence. "Crooked?"

Merv picked up his ashtray and unsuccessfully threw it at Danno's head. "You be fucking careful what you lay at my door, you Mick fuck. Where's your evidence that I tried anything of the sort? You didn't get the belt 'cause you'd only fuck it up if you did. Simple as that."

Annie lay on the bed and watched one of the most famous

wrestlers in the world tear at his clothes. His body was a little softer than she remembered. The road, and time, were taking their toll.

Shane smiled at her and tried to hide the fact that various injuries wouldn't let him get down far enough to take his socks off.

The hotel room, the running around, the planning, the danger. Back home it kept Annie going. She cherished the flutter it gave her. But here, in reality, it made her feel sick. Danno was a good man. Solid. Timed. Predictable. A little boring. But good.

"I can't," she said as she whipped herself from the bed.

"What?" Shane replied.

"I can't," she repeated as she dropped her head in shame and made her way to the door. "I'm sorry."

"Wait, baby. What's going on here?"

"I'm sorry. I don't know what I'm doing."

She managed to break away from this once before. Things were getting better at home. She didn't know what made her say yes to see him again.

History and chemistry were a dangerous combination.

"You're the worst earning member of this council, Danno. I'd keep my fucking mouth shut if I were you," Merv warned.

Danno slowly sat down.

Merv reigned over the silence in the room. He wiped the froth from his mouth and watched everyone else's reaction, waiting to take on any more of this uprising bullshit. "In case anyone forgot the procedure in here, there was a vote taken on this decision, just like every time we have someone who thinks they have the next champ. So, please do me a favor and stop with the bleeding heart routine in here. I'm getting all fucking emotional."

Merv was right. There were nine men who all had a say in the secret ballot. Just that none of them would say anything different than Merv. He had just enough of them on his side with backhand deals and co-promoting perks that he never had to worry about losing a ballot.

"Anyone else like to say something?" Merv asked.

As small and as old as Merv was, the whole business knew that he had come to this business from another business. If that old cunt didn't want you around anymore, you'd stop being around.

"Well?" Merv glared at Danno. "Are we moving this meeting on?"

Danno hesitantly nodded. There would be no celebration, no victory speech and no blowjob from Missus Garland that night.

Merv, in turn, sat down also. "I was going to inform the meeting that Sal was going to tour your territories again this summer as champion. Boost your gates."

The other owners smiled and nodded at the scrap of generosity and everyone turned attentively to his next item. Everyone except Proctor King, who winked at Danno.

Business was about to pick up.

All the real meetings took place after the meeting. All the owners knew this but never said anything. The planning, scheming, the hush-hush handshakes, all took place an hour after everyone left to 'go home'.

This is when Merv Schiller, as chairman of the NWC, normally held court, cut deals and generally protected his spot.

Merv wasn't the only one who was at a meeting.

Danno's took place with an unlikely ally in Proctor King. They never had much, if any, dealings with each other in the past. Proctor's request for a meeting was unusual to Danno to say the least. He took it because he just didn't want to go back home a failure again. He didn't want to have that talk with his wife again. He couldn't. He was too old to be an 'also ran'.

So he waited in the restaurant.

For an opening night, this Old Spaghetti Factory sure was quiet. Danno read the menu for the second time at a table that sat under a big stained glass window. Right on time, Proctor walked through the front door and pointed Danno out to the waitress.

The one man who was without a meeting was Curt Magee.

Same old shit, same old fucking shit, he thought as he lowered another beer and wiped the foam from his white moustache.

He skimmed and re-skimmed the meeting from earlier in his mind. The way he had been spoken to. The disrespect of cutting a grown man out of his livelihood. He knew that they were all planning a meeting without him. Curt's territory was hurting more than most. He needed a slice of the money that old Merv was funneling off for himself. But he knew he wasn't in Merv's troop – or any other troop. That left Curt very vulnerable.

To keep your place at the NWC table you have to be valuable. Curt was just about out of any worth – within the NWC or his own goddamn house.

He squinted at the figure at the end of the bar. "Shane?" he asked himself.

At the other end of the Governor Hotel bar, The Sugarstick Shane Montrose was lowering shot after shot. Curt didn't recognize him at first. Partly because his sight was shot, and partly because he'd never been in a bar with Shane Montrose where the Sugarstick was so quiet and somber.

"Well, fuck me," Curt said as he walked closer.

Shane barely looked up from his glass. "Curt Magee, the famous owner from Texas in these United States of America."

Curt dragged up a stool. "What are you doing here?"

"Fishing. What do you think I'm doing in a fucking bar? I'm knitting a hat."

"Okay, I was only asking."

Shane downed another shot and slammed his glass off the bar. "How many wrestlers did you all fuck over today?"

"What?"

"At your big meeting. How many of us did you guys fuck over? Did you cut our payoffs some more or trade us like the fucking cattle you think we are?"

Shane slipped uneasily off his stool and clawed at his shirt – ripping all the buttons off. He then struggled to pull his tailor-made jacket over his head – but only succeeded in trapping himself.

"Fucking help me," Shane said in a panicked, high-pitched voice.

Curt grabbed the jacket and Shane burrowed himself backwards out of it.

Curt became more aware of the scene they were creating. "What are you doing?"

"Freeing myself," Shane replied as he unhooked his belt.

Curt grabbed his arm. "People are watching."

"Fucking good." Shane pulled away from Curt and fell into an empty table behind him.

Proctor didn't feel at ease in the restaurant, so he and Danno came outside The Spaghetti Factory and slid down the bank by the river. Now it was Danno who was ill at ease. There was no one around. That's what Proctor wanted. Danno – not so much.

"Nice view, huh, Danno?"

Danno tried to assess the situation and the geography without making it obvious he was doing so. He also watched the water's edge so as not to get his feet wet.

"What did you want to see me about?" Danno asked.

"I want to do some business that will make us both rich," Proctor replied as he inhaled. "Big money."

"Haven't you got an office or a phone for this kind of stuff?"

"Not this kinda stuff."

Proctor waited for Danno's response. It was like he was enjoying the power of watching Danno digest the broken information.

"Well?" Danno asked. "What are we talking about here?"

Proctor took one last look up the bank before gravitating towards Danno's ear. "I want to get you the belt."

Danno leaned back to recapture his personal space. "You were there today, Proctor. You saw the room go with Merv."

"Fuck Merv and those monkeys who follow him. I can get you the belt by the end of the month. That'll give you time to put a program in place for that giant golden goose you found – you lucky bastard."

Curt and Shane sat in a booth in the bar. Shane was wearing just his jacket, underwear, black knee socks and shiny dress shoes. This arrangement seemed to have calmed him.

"Merv got me," Shane said as his suckled on a beer bottle. "He said I was the greatest of all time. The best wrestler to never have the heavyweight title. I agree with him there."

Curt also nodded in agreement. Everyone knew the same.

Montrose continued, "Merv said he was putting together the biggest match of them all. He got me to leave Tanner and come with him to San Francisco. I moved the family. Laid down some money on a nice house, put my kid in a new school. It was finally going to happen for me. He promised me the belt. Now he's fucking avoiding me. He won't even book me on his cards."

It took Curt all of two seconds to figure out why Merv would keep one of the best of all time on the shelf. What Shane was saying clicked with what Curt heard at the NWC meeting earlier.

Merv had tried to sign Babu the giant from under Danno's nose. He was wanting to put together the most popular wrestler never to be champion, Shane Montrose, versus the new Giant. Montrose trained the giant, broke him into the wrestling business. Teacher versus student. Experience versus youth. The rightful champion versus the new unstoppable giant. It was perfect. It was also a gold mine.

"Does he have a contract with you?" Curt asked.

"You know how these things work, Curt. I'm fucked."

"Jesus."

"Things are not good. This piece of shit has me signed for three years."

Curt saw the opening he was looking for.

"Merv is a greedy pig. He wants to collect all the talent and put them on the shelf so no one else can have them."

"Yeah, well, the way you guys have this game stacked – we only get paid when we work. And I can't live on fresh air and hollow promises."

"What are you planning on doing with Merv?" Danno asked, not sure if he really wanted to hear the answer.

Proctor dodged the question. "Listen, I want that belt – we all do, but everyone knows you've got the guy for now. The other owners had already signed off on it, except fucking Merv clicked his fingers and frightened them back into line. When he's removed from the situation, you get the belt. And my reward for doing it is that you drop the belt to me next."

Proctor tried to read Danno's face. "I pay you two hundred thousand dollars upfront and another two when your giant does the job to my son in a few years time."

"A few years?"

"Yeah."

"Why a few years?"

Proctor offered his potential partner a cigarette. Danno declined with a shake of his head.

Proctor answered, "I'm going to be honest with you. If I had all my pieces in place now I would just do this and get the belt for myself, but … my son just went inside," Proctor said with some noticeable pride.

Curt and Shane sat side by side, both feeling cheated, both making little money and both thinking what a greedy little prick Merv was.

Curt made absolutely sure that no one from inside the wrestling business was around before he stooped into Shane's ear. "Why don't you come work for me?"

Shane looked at Curt skeptically. He'd heard that one before.

"Fuck Merv," Curt whispered.

Owners didn't talk like that about other owners. Particularly in front of wrestlers. Shane was drunk, but not drunk enough to not be worried that someone might hear.

"He's got my contract," Shane said.

"What if I could do something that made us rich?"

Curt knew that Merv was trying to have all the cake. Merv wanted to own Shane Montrose *and* the giant. Curt didn't consider himself that greedy. If Danno Garland had the giant then Curt could snap up the challenger now and cut him off at the pass. Half the box-office of the biggest match of all time was better than none of the box-office of the biggest match of all time.

Curt wasn't comfortable in the open. He signaled for The Sugarstick to follow him into the small hallway off the restrooms.

"I'll sign you. We'll make the match. You versus the giant. We get half and Danno gets half. We do the match all over the country. There's more money there than any other match."

"What about Merv?" Montrose asked.

Curt took a swig of his drink. His hands were shaking. They did that a lot when he got excited or angry. "I'll sort Merv. I'd be doing everyone a favor."

Proctor flicked his exhausted cigarette butt into the river. "We got a deal?"

Danno felt he needed a lot more time. It seemed to make total sense as Proctor laid it out so smoothly, but he knew this was as close as his mortal self was ever going to get to shaking hands with the devil.

"Danno?" Proctor's pitch raised, surprised that he had to chase an answer.

Danno opened his mouth to not only agree, but to get himself in even further with Proctor. Money and fancy under-britches were powerful motivation.

"On one condition," Danno said, the water now running over his feet.

"What's that?"

"I call the angle when the time comes."

Proctor smiled and offered out a handshake. He knew that Danno was a simple storyteller. In the end, the giant would lay down for his boy. Proctor and Danno shook hands.

"Deal?" Curt asked.

Shane warily thought about what they were getting into. Merv left him no choice.

"On one condition."

"What's that?" Curt asked.

"I work *with* you. Not *for* you. Partners."

Curt saw five more years of work left in Shane's faltering body. If he could pull off a deal with Danno they would be the five most lucrative years of all their lives. If he couldn't... Curt didn't even want to entertain that thought. There's only one match out there that made any sense. And Curt Magee was about to outthink them all for once, and own half of it.

"Deal," Curt said.

Shane put out his hand, "Don't you ever try and fuck me over, lie to me or cheat me out of a payoff."

"I won't."

"Cause I'll fucking kill you if you do."

Curt finished his drink. "Anything I should know before we do this?"

"Like what?"

"Just anything you think I should know."

Shane shook his head.

"Okay. Deal," Curt said.

Curt and The Sugarstick Shane Montrose shook hands. Professional wrestling was littered with bad handshakes but this particular one ranked at the very top.

Four days after the murder.

New York.

Shane slowly walked the backroom towards Danno with his head respectfully bowed. He didn't know who knew what – if anything at all. He'd hoped that the fact he was still walking around meant Danno didn't know.

He was petrified, but not coming would only make things worse. So there he was, like a shameful dog, walking across the floor at Annie Garland's wake.

"Sit down," Danno said without raising his head from thought.

Shane did just that, "I'm sorry about … "

"Do you know where Curt Magee is?" Danno asked directly.

"No, I swear to God. I swear on my kid's life."

Danno opened his hand and showed him a tangled ball of rosary beads. "This is what they gave me. They took her and put her in the ground and this is the receipt."

"I'm sorry," Shane said, trying to hold back his tears. "I'm sorry."

Danno broke his stare from the floor and lifted his head. All the other mourners were sliding past the 'respect' phase of the wake and moving into the louder, more drunken part.

"They get you when you're a kid," Danno started. "And they put all this stuff in your head about devils and fire and clouds and light. And I can't fucking shake it. I can't carve the bullshit that they put in there out of my head."

"Danno … "

Danno slammed his fist off the table. The whole room stopped dead.

"What are you looking at?" Danno asked the quiet onlookers.

The room continued with its conversations and dirty jokes. Danno leaned into Shane Montrose. "I knew and I … accepted."

"Accepted what?" Shane asked.

"None of your fucking lies," Danno said as he dropped the rosary beads. "Not today."

Shane drew a large breath and clasped his hands on the table. He leaned in closer. "I loved her."

Those words, this day, no sleep, no joy. Danno did nothing.

Shane continued. "I loved her and I respected her. And my heart is broke over what happened. I want to help you find Curt."

Danno watched Shane's eyes fill up with tears. He then slipped his gaze around the filthy, smoky room. Danno Garland and Shane Montrose were the only two in the room who really felt something for Annie.

"I'm ashamed of what I did. I'm ashamed and it makes me sick to my stomach. It wasn't meant to be… it just got out of hand. I'm sorry Danno." Shane grabbed Danno's hand and dropped from his seat to his knee. "I'm sorry."

The room tried to pretend it wasn't looking at the scene unfolding in front of the boss.

Danno wanted to kill him – he wanted to stand up and thrust his fingers into his eyes and overturn the heavy table on the side of his head. He wanted to stomp him and stab at him and choke him and bite his face. "Get up."

Shane looked up from his bended knee. "I'm sorry."

"Get up I said."

Shane warily rose to his feet.

Danno stood and addressed the room. "Curt didn't fucking do this on his own," Danno shouted as he turned one by one around his fellow bosses. "I want you all to hear me when I say this."

The room was deathly quiet. Danno couldn't have picked a more awkward and uncomfortable day or place to unload.

"My only business left is to make sure who did this to … " He couldn't bring himself to say his wife's name. "To make sure everyone. Every-fucking-person who was involved in this dies. Then I will gladly lay down and you vultures can pick away."

Danno looked at all the dropped heads in front of him. "For years you all wanted me to get my hands dirty. Well, fuck you – they're dirty now."

Danno swallowed his shot, threw his glass against the wall, and walked to the door. "I'll give a hundred thousand dollars to anyone who leads me to Curt Magee," he said before he left.

Joe Lapine shook his head in disbelief. There was only so big of a crack he could smooth over as Chair of the NWC. An outburst like this, in public, and in front of the wrestlers was sure to incense the other bosses.

"Did he just place a bounty? *In here?*", Tanner Blackwell, the Carolina boss, mouthed to Joe in anger.

Shane Montrose, feeling responsible for the breakdown, reached into his pocket. He took out a ball of hundreds and walked to the bar. "This is on me. All of it."

He wanted to see if it was possible to spend his guilt away. He had a lot of money and a lot of guilt.

CHAPTER FIVE

Ginny stood somewhere. He was dressed in a suit. He tried to wait. Waiting always helped the fog to clear from his head. He was confused totally, but at least had the advantage of understanding that's what was happening to him.

He found it hard to verbalize. A proud, old-school man like Ginny didn't feel like talking about himself at the best of times.

This was not the best of times.

He waited for some familiarity to come back to him. Something to latch onto and make his anxiety pass and leave him.

"Sir?" boomed a voice from the other side of the door.

That voice wouldn't go away. It was in fact getting more impatient.

"NYPD. Open the door," demanded the voice outside before knocking on the door aggressively again.

For six hours Ginny lay on the floor. He remembered and forgot just why he was there. For a man as tough and as strong as he used to be, Ginny never felt quite as scared in his whole life. He was lying on the floor of someone's house for no reason, with no memory of how he got there. He was lying on the floor of his house for no reason, and with no memory of how he got there. The overbearing feeling of horror and not knowing what he was afraid of. The anger at finding himself afraid of nothing. The shame of not being able to do anything about it.

He lay there just wishing for Ricky to come. He lay there not knowing if anyone loved him. He lay there like a child lies quiet in their bed.

All he knew to do was just lie there. A scared stranger – in his own apartment.

Ricky Plick walked on West 42nd and stopped at a mid-sized, familiar building. The sun was high in the sky over the Island and Ricky had a long day ahead of him. He knew Danno's eye was off the ball so it was up to him to erase all the incriminating breadcrumbs leading back their way. Especially after Danno's announcement at Annie's wake.

If the bosses weren't out to get him before, they sure as fuck were now. No single owner can put out a bounty on the whereabouts of another without it raising eyebrows. Regardless of what happened.

He crossed the doorway of the building and pulled his collar nice and high on his face. He took the elevator to the third floor and walked the corridor littered with offices. He stopped at a door he rarely entered.

New York Booking Agency.

Danno's office.

Ricky moved the key he took from Danno's very slowly and quietly around in the lock and checked his back before entering.

After what Danno had done to Proctor, and how recklessly he had done it, Ricky needed to make sure that he disappeared anything that could catch them out. Anything that could lead anyone back to Danno.

That was his job. That was who he was as a person. Ricky was loyal and was looking after his boss's best interests even when his boss wasn't.

He opened the office door and navigated the room. He would have preferred to do this type of thing under the cover of darkness, but he didn't have that luxury.

Even though Ricky visited this office before, he never did so with an empty bag on his back and a stolen key in his pocket. He was certainly Danno's number two – but he stayed far away from 'the paperwork'.

This office was the place that made Danno *officially* who he was. To exist in New York, and stay under the radar, Danno had to run a real company. He had to have the papers to say that he owned what he owned. He had contracts with TV companies, wrestlers and the venues. He had to prove he paid taxes. That he had employees. His company was listed to this address, under his name.

That was the official bit. *The front.*

Then, behind that, was the *actual business.* The cash money, under-the-table business that he ran with the other bosses. The actual business fixed matches and bribed anyone who could make that pursuit easier. Wrestlers got cash under the table as well as fellow bosses, local TV owners, the guys that ran the buildings, some newspaper guys, a fire chief or two and a couple of cops from Danno's father's day.

That was a lot of money moving backwards and forwards. Everyone in the wrestling business was connected through a web of paper, IOU's, contracts and deals.

The phone rang and an answering machine kicked straight in. "Hello, you have reached the New York Booking Agency, the home of the world's greatest wrestling attractions. We are unable to come to the phone right now so please leave a message and we will get back to you as soon as possible. Thank you."

Beep.

The caller hung up.

Another thing Ricky learned down through the years was how to pay close attention from the side of his eye.

Danno's office was at the end of the room. Ricky pushed the door open, entered and quickly knelt down at the side of the huge desk. He took a paranoid little look before pulling back a thin rug. He then popped his finger down the inconspicuous hole in the floorboard and gently pulled. A perfect square lifted with him and exposed a built-in safe.

Ricky turned the numbered dial in a few different directions and opened the thick metal door. Danno trusted Ricky and never tried to hide the code from him.

Ricky's bag was already open and waiting. He removed five thousand dollars and placed it in the bag. Even with the money removed, Ricky saw that there was plenty more waiting in there. He figured maybe seventy or eighty thousand.

He quietly returned everything back to where it was and fixed the thin rug back in place. Ricky then stood and walked lightly out of Danno's dark office with a short stack of Danno's money for insurance.

If Ricky couldn't talk Danno off the road he was on, he was at least going to try and cover the tracks he was leaving behind.

Nevada.

Lenny guided his children, Luke and James Henry, across the parking lot of their motel. Luke had the ability to wander but James Henry still needed carrying over distances. Lenny also had a third item that needed careful attention – his wrestling magazine.

A couple of days previously, Bree was coming to California to live with her folks. She and Lenny were done. She had enough of his job. Lenny was a father to two young boys who barely knew him. The wrestling business kept him on the road for weeks at a time –

while his wife waited for him to come home. Sometimes she wouldn't even know where he was, if he was dead or alive. At the beginning that used to tear her up – at the end she didn't care one way or another. Nothing creates apathy like distance and rejection.

Bree began to plan her exit. She took some of the money that was hidden in their shed and stashed it for herself. She had been at home with the kids while Lenny worked. She had nothing of her own to use to move out. So she used what she thought was their money.

But Lenny begged to come with them.

Bree Long was the only woman in history who ran away from her marriage and collected her husband along the way.

But Lenny was determined to make it work with his family. So he packed up the job he loved as a bottom rung driver to come to California with his family. He was just too full of pride to stay with his wife's folks. So in the motel they were until Lenny figured something else out.

He put the brown bag between his teeth and he rifled in his pockets for the motel door key – but the door was already open.

"Hello?" Lenny said as he slowly entered.

Bree was sitting on the bed in her casino uniform. She was only at her new job for a couple of hours and not meant to be 'home' 'til later. She had her head in her hands and was sobbing.

"What's wrong?" Lenny asked as he quickly knelt down in front of her. "Honey?" Lenny asked again, trying to get her to lift her head from her hands.

"It's my father," Bree replied through her tears.

Lenny picked up on the fact that she was reluctant to continue with the children right there listening.

"Kids, go and wait in the car," Lenny said as he passed the two-year-old into the arms of the seven-year-old. They both struggled to stay upright.

Bree interrupted. "You can't send them outside, Lenny. Jesus."

She wiped her face, got up and turned on the TV, cracked open the candy and had them both distracted and quiet in seconds.

Lenny tried to rub her back as she moved but only ended up in her way. "What's the matter with your father?" Lenny whispered.

"Mom said he's had a stroke. I rang them on my break and she was just home to get some of his things."

"Jesus, that's terrible," Lenny said as he tried to embrace her. Bree was already throwing things into a bag.

"I've got to go," she said.

"Where?"

"To my folks, Lenny."

This could be perfect timing. Lenny could surprise Bree when she came back with the plan *he* was formulating.

"Okay," Lenny replied.

Bree stopped and looked at her husband. "I've got a friend who said she would watch the kids."

"They can't go with you?" Lenny asked.

"I can't bring the kids to see their grandfather like that."

Lenny muttered, "Has he got the face thing?"

Bree nodded. "Yes, he's got the face thing. I'd have to drive a couple of hundred miles out of my way to get to her first."

Bree wished Lenny was capable enough to step up and be a man.

"You should go," Lenny said. "You should do the right thing here. I could ... I could watch the kids."

Bree wasn't sure at all. She hadn't seen her friend since high school and she wasn't sure what kind of person she was now. On the other hand, Lenny had no experience of being a father.

Lenny slowed Bree down and looked her directly in the eyes. "Do you want time with your folks or not? I can follow you with the kids in a week or so. No big deal. It'll give you time, and your Dad time, and your Mom time, to focus on recovery."

Bree just wanted to go. If she left now she could be there in a couple hours. "You sure?"

Lenny nodded. "Of course. Jesus. Just go and ... help him."

Bree dried her eyes and hugged her husband tightly. Because of his previous job his kids barely knew him. She thought that was a good thing and she thought that was a bad thing.

"It'll be for the best. We'll follow you when you're all up to it," Lenny said.

"Lenny?"

"Yeah?"

"I'm kinda afraid that you're going to leave them on a bus or something."

Lenny kissed his wife. "I promise not to bring them on a bus."

Bree continued to pack for home. She wasn't the only one going home.

January 21ˢᵗ 1969.

Three years before the murder.

Memphis.

Today was the day. Curt Magee was going to get him some. He worked out a provisional fifty-fifty split with Shane Montrose, with a hundred and fifty grand upfront for his services as the top draw in his territory. Mrs. Magee didn't agree with putting their house on the line. *But fuck her.* It's not like they were together anymore anyways.

For once in his life, Curt felt smarter than all the other bosses. Danno may have the champion but he can't go out there and wrestle himself. All Curt had to do was remove his biggest obstacle, Merv Schiller, and the challenger in waiting was his.

So he waited at the end of Thomas Street. He wasn't quite sure how the plan was going to go. He was meeting a man his cousin put him onto for the first time. Thomas Street was a bad part of town and he had to meet a stranger with a pocket full of money.

Most of the other bosses were former wrestlers or college football stars. Curt, like Danno Garland had no such pedigree. That's why he brought along a handgun for company in case this all went to shit.

He watched his side mirror for anyone approaching. There was that silence that you can only get from an empty street. He waited as his bladder played games with him. He'd been for a piss twice.

The eventual sound of metal tapping on glass nearly made him shit his pants.

"Are you the guy?" a voice asked from the outside.

He composed himself and rolled down the passenger window a little. "Yeah, I'm the guy," Curt answered with his hand over his face.

"Gimme the money."

Curt watched Merv step out from the American Sound Studio. He took a bag of cash from his glove box and pushed it through the small crack in the window. "The old guy. Up there."

"Him outside the studio?"

"Yeah."

Curt and the hired hand looked up the street at the little old guy hanging off the end of his huge cigar. He looked frail and harmless and no trouble to anyone.

"You don't know him. He's a fucking … asshole," Curt said.

The man outside began to laugh. "Man, I don't give a shit. You say he's the guy, then he's the guy."

The man moved away from the car and reached inside his coat as he approached an unsuspecting Merv.

Merv flicked the cigar butt and turned toward his driver who had just taken the corner at the end of the street. He clasped his hands under his armpits and danced on the spot until his head was cracked open by a tire iron from behind.

"Holy fuck," Curt muttered to himself. He knew what was going to happen but he was still shocked to see it actually happen.

Merv's car stuttered to a stop and his driver ran towards his boss. His fresh, plentiful blood surged along the ground and pooled beside his gloved hand.

Curt sat in darkness a few hundred feet away. He turned on the ignition calmly and rolled his car back without any lights on. He didn't think of prison or he didn't think of Merv's family. He drove towards the other end of Thomas Street in Memphis, Tennessee and he thought about money.

Four days after Annie's murder.

New York.

Ricky covertly took Danno's used .38 Special from his pocket. Ginny had told him that cops came knocking but he couldn't remember why. And he didn't know when. It sounded close. Too close. So Ricky threw Danno's used gun into the dark waters of the Hudson in front of him.

Gone was one piece of evidence from the night Ricky wanted to never remember again. He only had one more piece left to get rid of. And he was holding five grand cash in his car to make sure that large piece of evidence was taken care of too.

He rested his forearms on the railing and filled his lungs with air and his eyes with the city. He liked it best at a distance, so he could appreciate the sight without the noise. Each window made him think of someone working late or a deal being done. Money changing hands. People running for the elevator with the straps of their briefcases in their mouths and papers falling out from under their arms.

The buildings, the lapping water and the muted mayhem across the river. Brooklyn Promenade gave him a sense of perspective on Manhattan and other, more personal things.

"How much higher can they build those fucking things?" Joe Lapine asked as he stood beside Ricky and looked at the city across the water.

Both men focused on the two new identical structures which now dominated the cityscape.

"They're done. The tallest in the world," Ricky said and bit into his homemade sandwich. "A hundred and ten stories."

"Who the fuck needs a hundred and ten stories?" Joe asked like the visitor he was.

Ricky watched Joe survey the area.

"He's not here," Ricky said of Danno. "And we're taping our TV shows in a couple of hours so I have to get out of here soon."

No one else was there. Both men had the place to themselves, to speak openly.

"How is he doing?" Joe asked about Danno.

"He's good," Ricky said, lying through his teeth.

He walked back from the railing and sat on one of the wooden benches near the bushes. Joe sauntered across too.

"How's business?" Joe asked.

On that one, Ricky couldn't lie. "Not great."

Joe Lapine was appointed Chair of the NWC by Danno when Merv got killed. Danno wanted the belt, money and extra territories - but taking The Chair after Merv expired would have put Danno in the frame as the man who ordered the kill. So, Danno asked Joe, the seemingly level-headed boss in Memphis, to keep the seat warm until things calmed down.

But things never calmed down.

It was a deal that suited both men. Joe ran the meetings and took the collective business while Danno had the power and money of being the boss with the champion.

"There are concerns for everyone involved. The other bosses are still over there," Joe said nodding to the city. "And nobody is happy."

"He's the man, Joe. He's got the belt and he's got the territories. The rest of you are going to have to give him time to get back on his feet."

Ricky stood up. "Do you mind walking?"

Ginny was waiting for Ricky in their car and Ricky didn't want to leave him too long. Both men began to stroll.

"They've called a meeting at twelve tonight. They want to hear your plans. We even have the foreign bosses asking what's going on. In a chain like ours, one of us could pull the rest down with him. You know this as well as anyone."

"I understand."

"There's a trust issue forming," Joe said.

Ricky stopped and laughed at the suggestion. These bosses trusted each other not a single inch for a single second. They all knew the business. They sat in a tight circle and every one of them had a bare neck and a sharp blade.

"Danno's got it under control," Ricky dutifully lied.

Joe blew into his hands and slapped them together. "I'm not like Merv. You should probably know that. I take being Chairman of the

National Wrestling Council very serious. Now, I know Danno has got the most turf *and* he has the champion. But my job is to make this thing we have fair and equitable for *all* involved. Your business is a mess right now. And Danno's thing is at the heart of that."

"His thing?"

"His personal matters. It's all drawing a lot of attention our way. He's making accusations and threats against the other bosses. He should have never done the deal under the table with Proctor. The riot in Shea, the senator getting knifed ... Danno's wife. It's all coming from your territory."

How could Ricky argue? "We'll fix it."

Joe was adamant that Ricky hear everything he had to say. "We can't do our jobs if people employed by the government are looking too closely at us. Senators, The Athletic Commission, cops. We need this to go quiet. Let this all pass without any more fucking incidents."

"Is that what you'd do?" Ricky asked. "Your wife comes up dead somewhere and you'd just drop it for the good of the business?"

"He got his peace. We all made sure of that," Joe said, reminding Ricky of Proctor's demise only the night before. "He has used up all his rope on this matter. You'd be wise to let him know that."

Ricky listened carefully. He couldn't argue with anything that Joe, as Chairman of the NWC, was saying. He just had a feeling that Joe mightn't have anyone else's best interests at heart.

"He's got this Joe."

Joe had heard enough. He buttoned his long overcoat up to his neck.

"How much longer do you think the other bosses are going to allow this to go on?" Joe asked. "For a hundred years we've tip-toed around, made our money and kept to ourselves. We're fucking promoters. We're not in the killing business. If someone has an issue with someone then they need to sort it outside of our deal. If someone needs to be taught some manners or something, we do it amongst ourselves and we do it for the good of the business. Danno is intent on placing a powder keg in the middle of our livelihoods and he don't care what the outcome is. If he doesn't pull back it's going to arrive at all of our doors. Don't make me do something about this."

Joe walked away.

CHAPTER SIX

Three years before the murder.

New York.

Curt couldn't believe the difference. The driveway, the grounds, the house, the jealousy. He was convinced that all he had to do was wait his turn. And negotiate himself a better deal.

That's why he was there.

That's why he turned up to Danno's new house a day before all the other bosses. He'd blame the mix-up on his secretary. All to get the new Kingpin's ear first.

In the driveway was a simple black Sedan. Danno never did get another personal car after his brand new Cadillac got suspiciously burned out in front of his old house. He just hired himself a greenhorn named Lenny Long to take him places instead.

Curt parked his car nice and neat – left Shane Montrose in the car – and took the walk up to the open door. A young, skinny figure walked out to nervously meet him.

"Is Mr. Garland in?" Curt asked the rookie driver.

Lenny looked back over his shoulder and waited for direction from the hallway.

"Yes, sir. He is. Come on in," Lenny said as he stepped aside.

Curt tentatively walked into the house and took in the vastness of it. The stained wooden floors and the sweeping staircase.

Lenny, in turn, exited and drove off in the Sedan.

"Come in Curt," Danno called from the room to Curt's right.

Curt followed the voice and peered around the door. Danno was standing, looking out the window, with his hands clasped behind his back, puffing on a cigar. The room was empty, with high ceilings and classic moldings on the walls. It was such that every word bounced around and echoed on its way back out the door.

"Well, fuck me Danno. You've got some place here," Curt said.

Danno couldn't contain his huge smile as he agreed with the Texas boss' sentiment with a nod of his head.

"Where is everyone else?" Curt asked while already knowing the answer.

"We're all scheduled to meet tomorrow."

"Tomorrow? You sure?"

Danno nodded and moved away from the window. "Positive."

Curt offered Danno a gift. "For Mrs. Garland. I hope she likes crystal."

Danno took the present and thanked his visitor for his kindness.

Curt rubbed his tanned brown brow in fake confusion. "Shit, I was told to be here today. I'll have to fire her. I hired this honey from college. She's nice to look at but she has a memory like a goldfish."

"Let's take a look around," Danno said as he left the room.

Curt followed. "Old Mrs. Bollard used to have the memory of an elephant. Unfortunately she had the ass to match."

Curt laughed. Danno didn't.

Danno and Curt walked the land at the back of Danno's new mansion. Curt finished taking down Danno's new number into his personal pocket book.

"You can't ride a horse," Curt said.

"Why not?" Danno asked.

Curt looked at Danno's growing gut and tried desperately to walk back his previous comment.

"Cause you can't put yourself in danger now that you've got the champion."

Danno admired Curt's attempt at a complimentary cover-up.

"I'm serious," Curt continued. "You've got the golden goose now Danno."

Danno stopped. "What can I do for you Curt?"

Curt had spent the few minutes listening about bushes and trees and stables and fish ponds, all the while trying to take Danno's temperature. Was he in a good mood? Was now the right time?

"Curt?" Danno prodded.

Fuck it. No time like the present.

"I admire the way you came from the Council and took what you felt you deserved," Curt began. "I want to do the same."

Danno dropped the moist end of his cigar on the pristine lawn and stomped it into the soil. "Thanks for the compliment. But that sounds like you're planning to overthrow me."

"No, I want to follow your lead, Danno," he said. "I want to do business with you. Big business."

Danno picked bits of renegade tobacco from the tip of his tongue. "Let's hear it."

"I got The Sugarstick," Curt said as he whipped the contract

70

from his inside pocket. He could hardly hold his excitement as he galloped headlong into the speech he had rehearsed a hundred times.

"We take your monster and put him in a match with his mentor – the man who brought him into this business – The Sugarstick Shane Montrose. Your guy is the unbeatable savage that no one can stop. My guy is the white-meat babyface that has never gotten the belt. We pick the biggest venue we can get our hands on and make us a ton of money."

Curt purposefully left a break for Danno to chime in. He didn't. So Curt had to be more direct. "What do you think?"

Danno didn't need to think. "Probably not."

"What?" Curt cautiously asked.

"I can't sign my guy up for that," Danno said with a new confidence in his business dealings.

The visiting Texan stumbled over his words, "Why ... but ... "

Danno continued. "I've got the giant signed up for something in the long run."

"You're not sending your champion down to Texas?"

Danno knew that he couldn't politically cut Curt out. Danno was too new to make such a big play. Yet.

"No, I can send the champ down if you like."

A small smile started to push its way back onto Curt's face.

"But it's not for a program," Danno said. "I can send Babu down there but he goes over strong. Your guy shows his ass - and in a squash too."

Curt heard loud and clear. Danno wasn't going to allow any series of hard-fought matches. He *was* willing to let Shane Montrose and the new champion lock up, but Danno wanted Babu to win easily and 'squash' Shane Montrose before the champion moved onto the next town.

Danno wanted Curt to make his new golden goose, Shane Montrose, to look like a pussy. This would give Curt a once-off payday – but would kill his territory.

In wrestling there are two ways to lose. You can lose by the skin of your teeth and have people salivating for the rematch – or you can get destroyed by an unstoppable monster and be yesterday's news. If Curt's top star had to 'show ass' for the champ who was passing through, Curt would have a real tough time selling tickets with Shane's name for the remaining years on his contract.

Sometimes getting the champion to town wasn't the best thing for a territory. Especially when the champion was being promoted as a 'kill-all' monster.

"We could do a couple of draws and then your guy goes over in the third match or something," Curt suggested, trying to clasp any shred of negotiation.

Danno again shook his head. "Babu is going to be undefeated and dominant until it's time for us to hand the belt to someone else."

"To who?"

Curt was beginning to get agitated. He had taken down Merv Schiller, the main impediment to Danno's run, and he was starting to get the sense that he was about to get nothing for it.

"I can't say. Not yet," Danno replied.

"You're trying to tell me that you're willing to leave a mountain of money on the table because you're tied up with someone else?"

Now it was Danno's turn to be annoyed. "Listen Curt. I can't be any clearer than this. I will send the champ to you. He's not losing. He's not going to look weak to an old, broken down guy like Montrose. My guy is the future. If you want him to come to your town you better have something more interesting that a squash match against a washed up has-been."

Danno's reply had a calming, sobering effect on Curt.

"I have been stupid here today Danno," he said. "This isn't my normal style. I know you're only finding your feet."

Curt put out his hand. "Of course we can do business. We'll think of something else. Something better."

Both men shook hands at the back of Danno's new mansion.

"Well?" Shane wanted to know as they pulled away from the house.

"Wait a second," Curt answered while checking his mirrors to make sure Danno couldn't see the anger in his face.

"You don't look good, Curt."

As Curt pulled from the house, onto the open road, he noticed the black sedan approaching from the other side. He shook the gloom from his face and smiled and tipped his hat as the car passed. Lenny, the driver, acknowledged him in return. The car's passenger, Danno's wife, was reading a paper and didn't notice the gesture.

Curt and Annie Garland would get the opportunity to meet again soon.

Shane covered his face as Annie's car passed. Curt noticed.

"You going to fucking tell me or not?" Shane asked.

"He didn't go for it ... "

Shane threw his hands up in frustration. "I don't fucking believe this man."

"He's not going for it yet. He wanted to do a meaningless thing where the giant comes to Dallas and pins you clean and leaves."

"Fuck no."

"Exactly."

The reality of the situation began to dawn on Shane. "I just moved my family again. Because you told me … "

Curt put a prepared envelope into Shane's lap. "I'm not like the other bosses. There's your first week's payoff."

Shane looked inside. "We didn't shake on payoffs. We shook on me being a partner in this deal."

"Okay partner," Curt said. "We made no money this week, would you prefer to split that with me fifty-fifty?"

Shane reluctantly nodded.

"I'll get this done. Meantime, that's some nice money in there."

Curt was right. The payoff looked thick and, as usual, Shane could sure use the money.

"I'm going to do a trade with Jose Rios … "

"In Mexico?"

Curt turned into a gas station. They were low.

"Yeah, I'm going to get his top star to come to us for a program and then you go down there and return the favor. You hungry?"

Curt opened his door but Shane grabbed his arm. "This isn't what we shook on."

"I can't make Danno pick us. We'll have to bide our time. While we're waiting, do you know how much we can make with a Mexican in Dallas?"

Shane wasn't happy but he knew the right Mexican name could draw big money. Not NWC champion money, but enough to live on for a couple of months.

"I want a Mexican Mexican. Not a Puerto Rican Mexican. I can't draw money against a Puerto Rican," Shane said.

"Okay. Now, can I get some gas?" Curt asked.

Shane wanted Curt to look him in the face. He wanted Curt to know that he wasn't to be messed with. Not this time. Not again.

He said, "I've had enough of being screwed around by you guys. If you try and fuck me over on this deal I will kill you."

Curt nodded. "We're going to make what I said we were going to make."

Shane backed off, his point was made and received. Curt patted down his pockets.

"Fuck," Curt said as he reached into Shane's open envelope. "I'll pay you back when we hit home."

Curt left the car and whistled as he walked to the kiosk. He didn't want to whistle, didn't feel like whistling. But he whistled. Whistling made the broken deal with Danno seem like no big deal.

But he knew it was.

There were boxes and bags and half-opened drawers. A TV sitting atop a makeshift stand of suitcases stacked one on the other. Danno and Annie eating from paper plates, across from each other. Just two people in a home made for more. A lot more.

He thought of all the shit he had to crawl through, all the decisions he didn't want to make. He wondered if she still loved him. He watched her watching TV. The smile on her face as she kept full contact with Debbie Reynolds. The way she leaned into her plate, with her food waiting on the fork until she stopped laughing.

Every now and then she'd flick her eyes over to him and smile – not waiting for him to return the gesture. She was happy. And the real kind of happy too. The kind where a person feels content.

A simple night, with a simple meal in a cobbled together setting in the middle of a huge, unpacked mansion.

Danno had finally gotten the power and the money. But he knew he was losing her. She, the one who he was sure he still loved, was sure he couldn't talk to, and was sure was having an affair.

He wanted to be angry. He wanted to be a man. More of a man. But he couldn't. He couldn't because he understood it. He could see the reasons why his wife, his rational, kind and loving wife, would cheat on him.

And 'cheat' was such a harsh word.

He was a young man when he married her. He promised her children and a certain type of life. She was shy and wanted nothing too explosive. They would talk endlessly about the life they were going to have and the plans they wanted to make. But when they were man and wife he bounced them around from city to city and became more quiet. Less inclusive.

She begged him not to get into the wrestling business. To stay outside with her and be someone other than his father.

Danno didn't listen. His younger head was far thicker. He had his beautiful wife with him and he found it frustratingly impossible to talk to her. He wanted to say things to her. He wanted to apologize for what he had become. He wanted to wipe it all away and start again.

He wanted to tell her that he loved her.

And all the years passed on by and he didn't talk to her. He didn't find a way. He didn't explain to her why he solely made the decisions that shaped her life. She never got what she wanted. Not even half, which would have been at least fair in Danno's mind.

He wanted her to be happy. And he wanted her to be with him. He wanted her to be happy and with him. But one didn't equal the other.

He knew why. It wasn't some mystical edict from the gods. It was him. It was his inability to explain, to confide in his wife. To tell her what made him afraid.

He planned with her, he married her and then he froze her out.

And still she could be happy as she was, sitting across from him. *She* was happy. They were not.

Danno stood up and walked around his wife to the door. Their new house was otherwise dark. The fire wasn't lit but the light from the TV made the room look warm. He stood behind her and he wanted to lean in and kiss the top of her head. He wanted to say sorry. He wanted to ask her to stop.

He wanted to, but he didn't do any of those things.

One month later. Three years before the murder.

Texas.

The Sportitorium was a white, barn-like venue that sat on the grounds of Industrial Boulevard. At one time it was one of *the* whistle-stop spots for blooding new up-and-coming recording artists before they became music mega-stars.

It was also Curt Magee's base.

Attendance had dropped hugely since those heady days of Johnny Cash and Elvis Presley singing in the center of a rope-less ring, but Curt felt they were on the verge of something. He could feel it in his bones that things were close to big-time again if he could just hang on. Hang on and make the match – Shane Montrose versus Danno's champion in New York.

"What the fuck is that?" Shane asked as he stepped out of his chauffeured ride into the splintering sun.

"That's Nelly," Curt answered as he walked out of his office to meet him.

"Nelly?" Shane asked, looking at the black bear tied to a tree.

Curt nodded and seemed to want to move quickly into the building and onto other matters.

"That's not for me, is it?" Shane asked, half laughing, half serious.

"We've got something for everyone tonight," Curt said. "I got a bear, some midgets, a few nice ladies and a gimmick match."

Wrestling fans loved the gimmick matches. They were the matches where the conventional rules of wrestling went out the window. There was the Bullrope Match where two wrestlers were attached by the wrist to a long rope which had a cowbell in the middle which could be used as a blunt weapon. Or the Texas Bunkhouse Brawl, which was a free-for-all type match that typically left both wrestlers drenched in each other's blood and the arena all torn up.

Tonight, Curt had booked a tar-and-feather match.

Shane was wondering if he'd just landed on another planet. "So, what am I doing?"

"There's a horse," Curt answered.

"I'm wrestling a fucking horse?"

Curt opened the door to the arena and motioned for Shane to follow him inside.

"No, you're not *wrestling* a horse. You're going to ride one down to the ring for your match later. I figured it would be a great way to introduce you to the fans here on your first night in. Give things a little local flavor."

Shane stopped dead in his tracks.

"What's the matter?" Curt asked.

Shane got a strong feeling that he was in the wrong place. He turned around and could see a scared teenage boy with ginger hair leaving an open bottle of beer within the bear's range.

"Go easy on me later, you hear?" the boy said to the bear from a safe distance.

Nelly the bear had just met her 'opponent' for that night.

Curt walked around Shane and into his line of sight. "What's the matter?" Curt asked again.

"I ain't no cowboy," Shane said softly.

Curt had spent all he had on this show. He even sold his car to pay for the animals. He needed his number one draw to be happy.

"We need to get you over with the audience. We need you to go out there and get them on your side the second they see you," Curt explained.

Shane couldn't have been more insulted. For any owner to tell an old pro like Shane Montrose how to get over with an audience was a slap in the face. Like telling a virtuoso how to play the piano.

"Have you ever seen me in the ring?" Shane asked.

"Of course I have. But down here it's different. Trust me," Curt answered.

"I've wrestled down south for most of my career. I know all about the southern fans."

Curt smiled. "You're not in The South. You're in Texas."

CHAPTER SEVEN

Four days after the murder.

Nevada.

Bree boarded her number nine bus. Her hastily packed suitcase was jammed tightly against her knees. It had already been dragged across the country, shoved in a motel wardrobe, only to be packed and dragged away again.

She was heading to Bakersfield to see she didn't know what. She looked out the window and watched her sons wave her off. Her stomach turned at the thoughts of them staying behind and waiting for her call. It also turned at the thoughts of Lenny being solely responsible for their collective well being.

"Goodbye," she mouthed through the hot, dusty window. "I love you."

Lenny's back was turned to the bus as he made a call at the station's payphone. Luke waved frantically as it was the first time in his young life that he was going to be away from his mother. He didn't really want to be left there at all. Lenny was more like an uncle that comes to visit than a father to him.

"We're going to fly in today, Mom," Lenny said down the phone.

"Me and your father won't be here, Lenard. We're going to head on down to your aunt Hendy's birthday party," Lenny's mother replied.

Lenny paused for a second to think.

"Why don't you bring the little ones there?" she asked.

"Can I?" Lenny asked.

Luke tugged on his father's shirt as Bree's bus pulled out onto the road. She was desperate to get his attention before she pulled off on her journey. She was waving like crazy and blowing kisses to her boys.

"Dad?" Luke said, trying to get Lenny's attention.

Lenny just shrugged him off and continued talking to his mother.

"You can come down to the Hendy's *with them* but I don't want you *dropping* them down there."

"Why not?" Lenny asked.

"Because your father and I want to have some cocktails and stay for a few days. Do you know how long it's been since we've been on vacation?"

Bree's bus was out of sight before Lenny realized his opportunity to say goodbye was long gone.

"Don't touch your father's car," Lenny's mother warned him.

"I won't."

"He loves that car Lenard."

"I know."

"What are you coming back so soon for anyways?"

A couple of years before, Danno gave Lenny a few grand here and there to stockpile in Lenny's shed.

It was a strategy that all the bosses used just in case they needed to get out of town in a hurry. They had money stashed everywhere. Or everywhere but a bank.

Danno showing such faith in Lenny had Lenny feeling like one of the inner circle. He was only too happy to take on the job. Not that he could tell his wife what he was doing.

At that time, Lenny was gone from his home weeks at a time and was so distant and secretive that Bree thought they were slowly separating. She watched her husband time and again sneak into their shed and hide money from her.

After a couple of years of lies and deceit, she had enough.

Her mind was made up and all she needed was some running away money for her and the kids. So Bree took a slice off the top of this 'hidden' money to set up a life somewhere else.

But then Danno called. He wanted his money. And quick.

When Lenny found out what Bree had done he couldn't make up the difference. He packed the remaining cash into a rucksack with a note of apology – and as an act of loyalty – Lenny put his wife's wedding ring set in the rucksack too.

It was all they had of value. Lenny wanted Danno to know that he was going to pay him back. The rings were just a temporary thing until Lenny got the missing money together.

But Danno never looked in the rucksack. He just handed it straight to his wife as she boarded a plane for Texas.

It was the last time Danno ever saw her alive.

"Lenard?"

Lenny was staring at the hill in the road. He hoped Bree's bus would come back so he could say goodbye to her.

"Lenard?" Lenny's mother shouted again down the phone.

"What?" he answered.

"What are you coming back to town so quickly for?" she asked him.

"I'm just coming back to collect something for someone. I'll just be a day or two."

Lenny had Danno's money. Now he wanted his wife's rings back.

Pennsylvania.

Allentown wasn't New York. And that wasn't a bad thing. But the Hamburg Field House wasn't Madison Square Garden and that wasn't a good thing. But it was better than where they came from. Philadelphia was one dangerous town to visit. The wrestlers loved the move.

The venue was a large gym with seats placed on the wooden floor. It was small and dingy but it would be full. Unlike The Garden.

It still had the painted white brick dressing room. The wooden benches. The chewing tobacco. The cards. The beers. The smoke. The ball breaking.

Like nearly every venue.

Backstage, two wrestlers were standing in their underwear, washing their ring trunks after fifteen days on the road. Everyone else 'washed' with a splash of Brut. A huge three hundred pound power-lifter was putting on his flowery shower cap to spare his newly dyed locks. More were shaving their body hair and putting on their face paint.

Huge scary men, getting ready for their audience.

Their bags were pungent. Their hangovers were worse. Some broke away from the card game to warm up in the corner. Another broke away to puke up the previous night's adventures.

These men were sore, beat up, tired, hung over, homesick – and ready to go again. Same as they were last week, last month and last year.

The show was never over for wrestlers. Any interviews or media appearances, or anytime they left their home – they were their wrestler's name and persona. Some of The Boys even stayed that way at home. 24/7. Protect the business at all costs.

They all knew the money was in making people believe. And some of The Boys didn't trust their wives and their big mouths to keep the con quiet.

Outside, Ricky hurried through the door. He needed to tape enough matches for a couple of weeks of TV. He then needed to get the wrestlers to cut interviews for different markets.

He also wanted to talk to Danno's giant star too. He had an idea that could see Babu, the seven foot, four hundred pound giant get his heat back – to make him the most despised wrestler in the country again.

All Ricky could think about was how to make the NWC come together again. He needed to get his work done and get back to the city to meet the other bosses. He knew this bad feeling couldn't go another day.

New York.

Danno stood outside a building with his finger pressed on the buzzer with no number.

"Fucking ... stupid ... fuck," Danno mumbled to himself as he stood back and looked up at the window.

"Troy?" Danno shouted.

Troy Bartlett was Danno's trusted lawyer. He moved paper around, sprung wrestlers from jail and kept anything illegal out of sight. He was on call all day, everyday. Danno never had to wait more than a half hour for him to return a call or make it to his house to discuss business.

It had been days since he'd last heard from him. He took out the note that was left under his door just in case he had missed something.

It read:

There's a heatwave coming up from Florida. You better cover up.

It was definitely Troy's stamped crest in the top right hand corner of the page.

Danno stood outside his shitty little uptown office and left his finger on the buzzer. He thought he was in the right place. All their previous business was conducted at Danno's place or on the road.

There was nothing. No answer, and it was getting late.

What the fuck is going on?

"Mr. Garland?" a coy young woman asked from behind.

Danno turned to see a slight, nervous-looking young woman getting out from a parked car.

"Who are you?" Danno asked.

The young woman took a cautious look around and walked closer to Danno. "Did you get my note?"

Danno watched her very carefully. "What note?"

The young woman was unsure of how much she could say on the street. "I left a note for you." She waited for Danno to give her a sign that he knew what she was talking about. He didn't.

"I asked you who you were," Danno said.

"I'm sorry. I'm Katy. I work here. We've never …"

Katy could see that Danno was clamming up. He didn't look too impressed with her explanation so far.

"I can let you in to see for yourself," she said as she fished out a bunch of keys from her purse and opened the office door.

"That's fine," Danno said, softening a little.

"He left two days ago and I haven't seen him since."

"What are you talking about?"

"He said he had to get away for a while," she said nervously.

"Get away from what?" Danno asked.

"You, sir. He said he had to get away from you."

Danno, and Katy Spence sat opposite each other in the diner across from the office. It was busy and loud. Waitresses glided around with plates and coffee pots as patrons struggled to catch their eye.

Usually Danno would eat half the menu and sample the other half. Today, he wasn't in the mood. And the parked car outside the diner was putting him off too.

Katy wiped the spilt coffee from her chin and Danno handed her a napkin.

"You seem very nervous," Danno said.

"I'm not cut out for this," she replied with the weight of honesty. Her brief seconds of truth were quickly covered over again with waves of anxiousness. "He frightened me with the way he was talking. He was paranoid and jumpy. Pacing around and biting his nails. Even at home *I'm* pulling the drapes closed in the day and I don't know why."

Danno wanted to see just who this woman was. "Why don't you write out that note for me now?"

"It just said … "

Danno stopped her. "I'd prefer if you'd write it down."

Katy nervously reached into her bag and took out a notepad and pen. He just wanted to make sure the writing matched the note that was left under his door.

Katy wrote and Danno could see in the first couple of words that it was indeed her handwriting on the note he had. He stopped her writing.

"Could he not just have called me?" Danno asked about Troy.

Katy was clearly uncomfortable with Danno's aggression. Danno caught himself and toned it down.

She continued. "Pardon my ... I don't know what to call it. My ... forwardness. And I love Mr. Bartlett ... but he wasn't thinking much about anything or anyone only himself. He just said that they were coming for you. That's all."

"Who's coming for me?"

Katy leaned in a little. "The police."

She opened her purse and rummaged around the end for some money. Danno could see that she hadn't got much. She was like his wrestlers. No work. No pay.

"He said that I should tell you to wrap all the loose ends up. Cover your tracks. Smooth over whatever it is you need to before the cops ... you know.... arrive."

Danno put on his tweed cap. "If he contacts you for anything, you make sure and get him to call me. You hear me?"

Katy nodded and pushed her coffee cup into the middle of the table with a slightly trembling hand. Her red hair reminded Danno of something. Something nice. Something good.

Danno tried hard to see who was sitting in the car across the street.

"Did he leave you anything?" he asked.

Katy shook her head.

Danno opened up a folded stack of notes that were held in place by an engraved money clip and ripped out a tidy bundle.

"No, I can't," Katy said, embarrassed.

"We don't know how long he'll be gone for, Miss. Take this to tide you over," Danno said as he put the money on the table. He was insistent but kind.

"Thank you," she said unable to look Danno in the eye.

"You should have all of this," he said as he reconsidered and left her the full clip of money.

Katy instinctively rose out of her seat. "No, no. I can't. Thank you though."

Danno left without hearing her argument. He wanted to pay the driver across the street a visit.

Pennsylvania.

Ricky sat on his own, going over the card for the next night. He knew the payoffs for The Boys were going to be rough in New York. They were all promised more after Danno got control of San Francisco and Florida.

It was to be the start of the super payoffs. Feuds and matches that could crisscross the country.

Ricky kept looping the 'careful what you wish for' sentence over and over in his head like some kind of karmic anesthetic.

Danno wanted New York, Florida, Texas and San Francisco. And he got most of them, but now they were Ricky's problem. He couldn't let such huge territories die on the vine and he didn't have the authority to execute any major plan on his own.

He was trapped in some kind of limbo. He could neither retreat or advance. Nor could he trouble his boss for a game plan.

The hall outside was packed with wrestlers who were full of questions and problems. Ricky just didn't want to talk to any of them. He only had one meeting on his mind. Not the type of meeting that he wanted to have – but one that he *had to* have.

"We need to talk," Oscar Dewsbury said as he pushed himself into Ricky's locker-room uninvited. "What is this shit man?" Oscar asked angrily.

Ricky waited silently for him to get to the point.

"They're telling me that I'm suspended. That fucking asshole from the Athletic Commission is saying that I no-showed a match in Fresno two nights ago."

Not so long before, Oscar Dewsbury left Danno Garland high and dry when he jumped from New York to the rival Florida territory. Unfortunately for him, Danno eventually got control of Florida – and Oscar Dewsbury.

"I have to pay a five hundred dollar fine too. How the fuck am I supposed to eat?" Oscar asked.

Ricky snapped from his deeper thoughts and drew a breath. "If you no-show, they do what they do. Take it up with them."

"I was in Tampa that night. Working. *You* fucking booked me to go there. Danno knows that. That's why he booked me in two towns and didn't tell me. Isn't it? He knew what he was doing. That fucking… "

Ricky quickly grabbed his massive visitor by the neck and slammed him against the cold wall. "You think with everything he has going on in his life right now that he took the time to fuck with you? You're lucky he's as lenient as he is. The way you screwed him over. Who leaves a man when he's down? Hah? You took the money and ran when things were tight up here. I would shut my mouth if I were you. Do you hear me?"

Oscar could feel Ricky's grip bending his windpipe and closing off his carotid artery. "Yes," he pushed out from the back of his constricted neck.

Ricky released him but struggled in not following up with a head-butt to punctuate his point.

"You fucking respect that man and everything that's going on for him right now," Ricky said of his boss.

Oscar rubbed his throat and tried swallowing normally.

"Now get the fuck out of here."

Oscar stumbled out the door and Ricky stood in the middle of the room. He had to roll the dice. He had to come up with something outside of the everyday. Ricky knew that if he didn't propose something to keep the other bosses happy then Danno was a sitting duck.

New York.

"Who the fuck are you?" Danno asked as he approached the open car window from the diner. The daylight was gone and the figure looked a little more mysterious sitting there half-light.

Behind Danno, Katy ran from the diner with her purse full of his money.

"I'm a cop," the man in the driver's seat replied. "My name is Nestor," he said as he leaned into Danno's line of sight. "Why don't you hop in here?"

Nestor Chapman was the kind of man who worked extra shifts, washed in a sink and had a natural tan that was carved nicely around his jet black mustache.

"I'm on a break," Nestor said as he showed Danno his Thermos and homemade sandwiches.

He was young, maybe early forties but wasn't wearing a uniform.

"Fuck you," Danno answered and walked the other way.

"You don't look so good, Mr. Garland. Are you looking after yourself since … you know, Mrs. Garland?"

Nestor opened his car door and stood, leaning on his car roof.

"What's your deal?" Danno asked as he turned back around.

"I'm a friend of a friend of yours."

Danno was just trying to figure out if his new admirer was being helpful to be helpful or being helpful to get information.

"And who would that be?" Danno asked.

"Why don't you get in so I don't have to do this on the street?" Nestor said.

"Are you arresting me?"

"I'm offering you a sandwich."

Nestor could see Danno thinking about it.

"I can't promise the sandwich won't hurt, but I can say the conversation won't."

He could see the doubt in Danno's face. Nestor suddenly realized how stupid it was to ask Danno to get in a car with a stranger, so he showed him his badge and his most trustworthy face.

"You're going to have to trust me here for a couple of minutes Danno," Nestor said as he drove and ate.

"You won't be offended if I don't," Danno answered.

Nestor enjoyed Danno's response. "No, I don't suppose I will."

"Why are you doing this?" Danno asked as they cruised down Empire Boulevard.

"I don't give a fuck if you make your money from throwing matches. It's not on my list of the shittiest crimes in this city."

"One of my guys would murder your whole boxing club," Danno replied with great offence.

"Alright old man. Whatever you say. I'm just saying. I don't want nothing from you. I'm not looking for you to tell me anything. Tip me off or anything else."

"Who's your friend that's my friend?" Danno asked after a slight pause.

"Let's just say that your legal counsel asked me to touch base with you."

"Troy?"

"I have no idea who you're talking about," Nestor replied with a smile. He lit up a cigarette and rolled down the window. "You need to start worrying about your own ass."

"And why's that?" Danno asked.

Nestor shook his head. "A US senator gets stabbed on a New York street and a whole lot of lazy, fat captains and police chiefs suddenly get motivated. You were sloppy, Danno."

"I had nothing to do with it," he truthfully replied.

Nestor turned his gaze straight ahead and packaged his next sentence as soft as he could. "They have one of your guys who says he'll talk."

Danno's stomach sank even further.

"He's coming in soon. Sounds like tomorrow night," Nestor continued.

Danno didn't react in the slightest.

"I don't know who it is yet. Only the higher-ups have a name so far."

Nestor stopped at some traffic lights.

"Let whoever it is come in and waste your time. I have nothing worth talking about," Danno said as he opened his car door. "And if any of you fucking people want to come arrest me, then you come see me. Until then … "

Danno left the car and slammed the door and began to walk. Nestor pulled up tight to Danno on the sidewalk and softly said, "When this guy comes and opens his mouth your room to maneuver is gone. If you have anything that you need to clean up or hide away, now is the time."

CHAPTER EIGHT

Two years before the murder.

Texas.

"What fucking else even makes sense?" Shane asked the stoic body sitting silently opposite him in the otherwise empty locker room.

Shane, completely naked, ran a long white line into his nostril and side fisted the wall with sheer adrenaline. "The fucking giant across the ring and the arena is full. I bump all over him, making him look like a fucking brick wall. He gets heat on me. Boom. Boom. ... I fucking slide to the corner with my hand up to heaven. He's fucking got me by my tights and just lifts me off the mat and whack, fucking head-butts me in the back of my head. I fall down like a puppet without strings. The place goes crazy and starts chanting my name."

Shane breaks from his story only to snort another line. He notices the expressionless face across from him but continues regardless.

"And then he makes a mistake. And I slowly fire everything I have at him. Wham. I hit him in the throat with a closed fist. I hide it from the ref but the people don't care because I'm the babyface and they'll let me cheat a little. I fucking chop-block his tree trunk leg and he starts to wobble. And Chrissy, that big giant fuck, is good at selling those too. He'll make it look like it's the first time in the world that he's ever been hit that hard before. And man, I start to feel it. I start to feel the people running through my veins. I hit the ropes and fucking whack that African nog across the throat with a clothesline. I mean stick it to him. And he starts to wave his arms like he's trying everything he can just to stay standing and I run and hit those motherfucking ropes again and fucking ba-bam him across the throat again. The people can see he's going and they will me to hit him one last time. Take this big fucker off his feet for the first time in his life. The giant is in shock that he's even wobbling. Never happened before. And I hit the ropes as hard and as fast as I can and ... spadoink... he catches me in the fucking chin with a big boot and I go down like someone in the nosebleed seats just fucking shot me. And I'm lying on my chest hiding my face and I'm thinking. I fucking got you man. I got you fucking marks to cheer and believe that I could win this time and you fucking backed me and I got a fucking boot in the fucking face so fuck you. Miracles don't happen and giants don't fucking get taken off their feet. Until the next time I make a comeback and make you think the same thing again. That's my job, you see? I get them to pay money to see me win. And then fuck them. Hah? And I go to the next town and do it all again."

The man stood up and slid a small brown bag along the dressing room bench.

"Hah?" Shane said again, waiting for some response. "What do you think?"

"That's thirty-seven thousand owed in total. See you next week," the uninterested man said as he shuffled out of the dressing room.

"That's no problem," Shane replied, almost offended that the moneylender brought up the subject of money at all.

The man took out his book and penciled in the new amount. "I'll be back in two weeks to collect, plus interest."

"No problem," Shane replied, even more offended now that he mentioned the money again.

"What they do if you don't pay is – they break the small finger on each hand and double the repayments for twice as long."

Shane felt the need to cover himself up now. The atmosphere wasn't a pleasant place for his penis to be hanging out.

"Okay," Shane said in a suddenly serious voice.

The man left.

Shane sat in the front bleacher with ice strapped to his knees and both shoulders. He was sweaty and too tired to move from the seat. The Sportitorium was empty and covered in trash.

Shane smoked, not in any rush to get home.

"Hey," Curt said as he entered through the tunnel.

"We need a new ring. That one is covered in mildew. And it's like a rock," Shane said.

Curt hovered but said nothing.

"What was the house?" Shane asked.

"It was better. Looking like nearly a thousand paid."

Curt sat down in the seat next to Shane.

"That's still terrible," Shane said. "I'm working my ass off out there. I want an ass every eighteen inches out here. No empty seats."

"The house here is slightly better, but TV … there's a problem."

Curt's words got Shane's fullest attention. The wrestler knew that having local TV was the biggest marketing tool the wrestling business had. Any trouble on the TV side of the business meant trouble across the business as a whole.

"What's wrong with TV?" Shane asked.

Curt was clearly tired. Worn out.

"There's some internal dispute at the station over there. Something about ownership. Nothing to do with us," Curt said.

Shane could smell bullshit. "What dispute?"

"They're not really saying."

Curt lit up a smoke of his own. He rubbed his tired eyes and wondered what was keeping him in this business at all.

"They seem okay with not collecting our money every month," Curt said shaking his head.

"If we got no TV then we're finished," Shane said as he turned directly to his partner.

"Now, we're not done yet."

Shane tore the tape from his icepacks and let them fall on the floor. He picked up his bag and propelled it angrily towards the ring in frustration.

"What's really going on here?" Shane demanded to know.

Curt took a second before answering. He wasn't used to talking to wrestlers like this. But Shane needed to know what was on his mind.

"I think it might be Danno Garland."

"What?" Shane asked.

"I think he might be paying the station here to keep us off the air."

Shane stood up. "He's paying them to *not* have us on air?"

Curt nodded. "I think so. Looks like he's trying to starve us down here."

"Why the fuck would he do that?"

Curt in turn stood up and looked his partner in the face. "I have no idea. It seems he really don't like us for some unknown reason."

Curt stood on his cigarette butt and walked back to the locker rooms.

New York.

Ricky returned and took the steps into the shitty backroom where Annie's wake was held earlier. He wasn't surprised this was where they chose to meet. The greedy fucks probably got a special rate on the place. There was always an angle with the bosses.

"Gentlemen," Ricky said as he approached along the sticky floor.

Most of the bosses were still huddled in the corner. All the wrestlers were gone. There was only a circle of Scotch, chewing tobacco and cigar smoke left.

"Where's Danno?" Tanner Blackwell asked.

"*I'm* here," Ricky replied.

His response seemed to anger some in the circle. A few of the bosses threw their hands in the air in exasperation and sighed their disapproval.

Ricky knew he needed to pull the bosses back into the conversation quickly. "I'm speaking with Danno's full permission and on his behalf. I don't think it's unreasonable to give the man some more time to grieve."

"Thanks to all the shit you guys are pulling up here, we don't have fucking time for grieving," Tanner shouted. "The walls are moving in quickly on us."

Joe Lapine spoke softly from the head of the table. "Give the man a chance to speak."

The circle widened out and the bosses sat shoulder to shoulder in silence and waited for Ricky to begin.

"I need your help," Ricky began.

Tanner smiled at the predicament Danno, through Ricky, found himself in. One week before, Danno looked immovable as the top man. Now his number two was at the meeting looking for their help.

How quickly things can change.

"What are you asking for Ricky?" Joe asked. "What's your proposal?"

Ricky continued. "I want to open out The Garden to your guys. I want to run an elite tournament that would put all of our top guys in there. Proctor has run off somewhere – afraid to face the giant. We strip him of the title … "

Tanner again chimed in. "What the fuck does that do for us?"

Ricky wanted to launch himself across the table and beat Tanner's face in. He instead steadied himself and continued. "We take a new path. One with more room and more money. We tape this tournament at The Garden tomorrow. Then we all use the same footage on our local TVs. All your guys will look like a million dollars fighting for the biggest prize in wrestling, in the most prestigious venue in wrestling. We'll make your guys look like stars."

"But there can be only one winner, Ricky," Joe pointed out.

Joe's point had some nodding along in agreement.

Ricky shook his head. "No. Two."

"How the fuck can two win?" Tanner asked.

Ricky composed himself and continued. "In the main event we have a double pinfall. Both wrestler's shoulders on the mat at the same time when the referee counts to three. We have chaos and both men leave claiming the title of Heavyweight Champion of World. One for us here in New York. And one for whoever you decide. Then both men crisscross the whole country for six months calling themselves champion. Never a day off. Two matches on Saturdays and two on Sundays."

With every word, Ricky could feel the room moving his way. The body language was different. The hecklers silenced. Ricky could see that his proposal was sinking in well with most of the room.

He continued, "We all get twice the money that one champion can bring us. We all work together to get our business back on track, and we all make good out of it. Then at the end of six months we put them together and sell a super-bout for the ages. Two world champions clashing to decide who is the real world champion."

Joe tried to read the room from the side of his eye. He thought that Ricky might just have found a perfect win/win scenario to put his members at ease. All but one.

"Why six months?" Tanner asked.

"Because I want Danno to have the say in who ultimately wins and claims the unified title again. It's his belt to hand over if he wants. Or to keep if he wants. I just want him to have time to come back to the table."

Joe stood up from the gathering and walked towards Ricky.

"Thanks," Joe said as he escorted Ricky to the door.

Tanner stood too. "Wait."

Ricky and Joe stopped and turned around.

"What about Danno putting out a bounty on Curt Magee?" Tanner asked. "Not in the history of our great business have I ever heard of such a fucked-up move from one boss to another."

"We can't have that," Joe said in support of Tanner's question.

"I'll talk to him," Ricky said.

"Talk to him?" Tanner asked.

Ricky nodded his head.

Tanner wasn't happy at all with Ricky's softly, softly approach. "No. You fucking *tell* him that if he does anything else to draw attention to this business then all the talking stops."

Ricky studied the room to see if the rest of the bosses thought that Tanner's threat was out of line. Apparently, it wasn't.

"I understand," Ricky said as he turned back for the door.

Joe walked with him through the door. Both men stopped at the top of the stairs, out of earshot.

"Where does Danno want the other champion to come from?" Joe asked.

"Tanner," Ricky quickly answered.

"Tanner?" Joe asked.

Ricky shrugged his shoulders and nodded his head. "Yeah, Tanner is giving up Curt."

"What?"

Ricky buttoned up his coat. "Tanner is taking the bounty. He's meeting Danno tomorrow to give up Curt's whereabouts and to collect the cash. Danno wants him to have the second champion."

"Alright," Joe said, well aware of his duty.

Ricky put out his hand. "We need to get this going now. I have everything lined up at The Garden. I hope you can get this done."

"Me too," Joe replied unconvincingly.

Both men shook hands and both men went to work.

Two hours previously and the music pouring from the speakers would have made the troop of wrestlers on the dance floor more than likely kill someone. Now, knee deep into the 'wake' they were drunk, stoned, horny and on a night off.

"Just the way Annie Garland would have wanted it," one of them noted sarcastically.

They were also heels. Bad guys. Not liked. The babyfaces went to a different club.

The Sugarstick Shane Montrose was a 'tweener.' A bad guy in

New York and a babyface in Texas. He was so good at his job that even the most ardent fan bought him drinks out of pure respect.

And he drank them. Every single one.

He also threw fistfuls of money into the air and watched all the women around him dive to their knees in an effort to scrape some notes from the floor. He laughed as they pulled at each other's hair and ripped at each others clothes.

He danced without any semblance of style, control or grace in the middle of the floor. The women were drawn to him and their men were just waiting to test themselves against the visiting 'fake' wrestlers.

Across the floor those same wrestlers sat in hope that the men would try and see how 'fake' they were. For them it would have been the cherry on the cake of a perfect evening.

Nothing bonds professional wrestlers like a huge brawl.

The Sugarstick turned and twisted and rubbed himself in unison with the music and the week's worth of drugs in his system. He floated and could hardly contain his joy at being alive. The rush of being there, in that room, with those people, listening to that song was overwhelming.

His eyes moistened with joy.

In a world of his own. He spoke to himself as his hips operated without instruction or oversight. From inside looking out he was warm and confident and content and happy and at ease and strong and irresistible and forceful and capable and wrapped in all things good.

From the outside he looked like a fucking lunatic.

An embarrassment. Someone who, without money and wrestling fame, would have been thrown out on his ass a long time ago. He looked like someone who should be home with his kids or grandkids.

Shane nearly choked on the emotion rising up his throat. He

reached out his arms to bathe in it. He spun enough to blur the room as he turned. He saw a head of jet black, perfectly pressed, long hair on each rotation.

He wanted to feel it.

So he clasped onto it as he pivoted clumsily and yanked the woman attached to it from her seat.

"Fucking greatness," he shouted as he pulled the screaming woman around and around with him. Her girlfriends shook him and punched and slapped too so as he might let go.

Shane was elsewhere. Somewhere where he wasn't the scumbag he knew himself to be. Somewhere where he wasn't crippled with guilt and flashbacks. Somewhere where he was the undefeated world champion.

Shane Montrose lay motionless on the brown carpet. The meager contents of his turquoise hotel room were tossed and tipped over, except the umber-colored bed which was still perfectly dressed. His window was open and the earth-colored floral curtains flapped in the breeze.

On the floor, Shane hugged the phone. Even in his drunken stupor, he begged it to ring. Just ring. For hours he checked the dial tone and rang the front desk to make sure the lines were good. He richly paid the disgusting guy on the front desk to monitor the phones all day and all night.

But wish as he did, no call came through. He left his hotel phone number everywhere he knew Curt went or might be.

The Hotel Monterey wasn't the usual standard that the Sugarstick liked for himself when he was on the road. But when he left for New York he didn't know if he was going to be there for a night or a week.

Either way, he felt he had to be where people wouldn't think to look. Just in case his problems from home fancied a trip to the Big

Apple.

Ring, goddamn it.

He impatiently banged some numbers on his phone and waited. A sleepy female voice answered. "Hello?"

"Hey honey, any messages yet?" he said in his fake-sober, chirpy voice.

"Shane?"

"Anything from your brother?"

"There's nothing over there. He's checking."

"Is he going to the house everyday?"

There was a slight confused pause. "What? Yes. He snuck on over there this evening. There's nothing."

"You sure he's doing what he says he's doing?"

"Yes. I want to go home Shane."

Shane did all he could to hide his frustration. "Are you sure he knows how to work the answer machine?"

"Yes. Blinking red light. He's checking the goddamn machine," his wife shouted back.

Shane couldn't believe his luck. Another night without knowing where Curt was. "You've got this number honey? Haven't you?"

Shane's wife was growing more and more anxious with every question Shane asked her.

"You've given it to me twice now Shane. Is there something else wrong?" she asked.

"Go back to sleep," Shane said as he waited for silence on the other end.

"When are you going to get these people their money? We can't keep doing this? These people are coming…"

Shane hung up the phone in the middle of his wife's sentence.

It really came down to two men. Joe Lapine as Chairman and Tanner Blackwell as chief opponent. The NWC was made up of many members across the world, but the power lay at the top only.

And now that Danno was weakened and distracted, that power was moving downwards.

Both Joe and Tanner knew that.

The two men faced each other across a small, round room service table. They were happy to leave the meeting and let their wrestlers spread out across Manhattan to drink and hit the nightclubs. Tanner even gave some of his wrestlers an extra hundred to break a few jaws while they were out.

It was always a good investment for the bosses to pay their guys a little more to be tough with the locals. It protected the business and made wrestlers the one group of people you didn't want to mess with in a bar.

The more people they could prove they were 'legitimate' to, the longer the deception could go on.

Joe and Tanner's plates were filled with half-eaten meats, vegetables and exotic desserts. These were the plates of bosses who were earning money. The hotel room made the same extravagant statement. A room too big and too pricey for the single man staying there.

But, that was wrestling. A con. A sleight of hand. A play, from the second their eyes opened 'til the second they shut. Everyone in the wrestling business knew they were taking the money from the paying public or the 'marks' as they called them. They knew they were conning them.

But they also conned each other. It was a perception con rather than a deception con. They all did it to each other all the time.

Even the bosses did it.

Joe Lapine and Tanner Blackwell sat opposite each other, out-ordering each other with room service. They arrived on separate chartered flights. Drove in separate limos and booked the finest rooms in the finest hotels in New York.

And they were both broke.

Not broke like a guy who sleeps in the alleyway broke. But broke for a rich guy broke.

And they knew, like all the other bosses around the world, that Annie Garland's funeral was the place to be seen. They called in favors to borrow expensive jewelry or pawned their second cars for pocket money. If you're not seen like a boss then you weren't seen *as* a boss. And to be seen as a boss you had to flaunt. Everything. All the time.

Tanner all of a sudden dropped his cutlery, like he couldn't take it anymore. "I don't know if this is the right time to be seen *closer* to Danno."

Joe put down his cutlery and wiped the side of his mouth before speaking. "Now is the *perfect* time to be closer to Danno."

Tanner had a little think before picking up his fork again. "Why do you say that?"

"There's going to be two champions coming off the card tomorrow night. Danno has got one and you could have one. If something were to go wrong with Danno, who do you think is next in line?"

Tanner couldn't hide his grin. "Why are you so adamant that *I* have it?"

Joe pushed his plate back completely and cleared the food from his back teeth with his tongue. "Danno has essentially triple the vote when it comes to the title. He has New York, San Francisco and

Florida. We have one vote. We're going to be a long time out in the cold if we don't take this gift now. I've got no one ready. I'm voting for this. And Danno's three. If you vote too then it's a done deal that I can present to the members as a fait accompli. With that, you get the other title."

Tanner was back to full speed in shoveling his food into his mouth. "If I link myself to Danno and he fucks me over ... "

"You know what the field is out there at the moment. You just have to decide if it's too hot for you. Let me know and I'll arrange someone else to ... "

"We should get another bottle of champagne," Tanner said.

CHAPTER NINE

Five months before the murder.

Texas.

Geraldine pulled the chicken from the oven and threw it, and the shallow pan it sat on, into the sink. "You fucking hot chicken," she said as she sucked on her burnt thumb. She had a tendency to be literal in her cusses.

She scraped the broken carcass from the bottom of the sink, and slapped it onto a plate, before dumping some half frozen vegetables around the broken bones.

"Curt?" she shouted through to the front of her house.

Because she didn't get an answer within two nanoseconds, she shouted the same again – only louder. "Curt."

"Yes. Jesus," Curt Magee replied as he walked into the kitchen with a beer in his hand. The more his business broke down, the more time he spent sleeping in his mother's house.

Things weren't great for Curt at home with his own family.

"Where's your friend?" she asked.

Curt knew. He just knew what she could be like.

"Don't," he warned her.

"What?"

"Don't."

Curt noticeably slowed down as he came to the window and peeked outside before walking to the table.

"Just who are you ducking?" his mother asked, wiping the anxiety of preparing a real meal from her forehead.

"No one. Nothing," he replied as he sat down at the table.

Geraldine straightened her Aztec print dress to hug her figure more. "Where did you say your friend was?"

Shane Montrose entered perfectly on cue and Geraldine blushed a little when she realized he was behind her. His little fingers were taped up and he was unshaven and unkempt looking. He still wore a great suit but it had obviously been slept in. His eyes were red and yellow and his usual radiating tan was overpowered by a sick grey tone.

This was not the same man who packed out venues across the country. Shane Montrose looked like a man who tried to keep up his appearance but could no longer afford it.

Grobie Magee, however, didn't give a fuck. He was still Shane Montrose.

"Thank you for your hospitality, Mrs. Magee," Shane said as he entered the kitchen.

"Call me Grobie," Geraldine said with a dirty smile. "All the wrestlers call me Grobie."

Curt saw how hard his mother was putting her old body out there and shook his head in disgust. Over the years he'd heard things about her in the wrestling business that made him sick to his stomach. Simply put, Grobie was a Ring Rat who liked to fuck wrestlers. She was infamous for it up and down the business. Shane Montrose was kind of like her missing card to complete the set.

"Where would you like me?" Shane asked, shamelessly flirting with practiced ease.

"A couple of inches up in my … "

"No!" Curt shouted as he pounded his fist on the table. "I'm sitting right here."

Shane and Geraldine silently conceded that Curt had a point.

"There's salt on the table," Geraldine advised her guest as she pulled herself back to civility.

"Thank you," Shane said as he sat at the table.

Shane's mere presence was enough to sicken Curt. He was only there because he'd heard through the grapevine that Danno was calling Curt with an offer. It was damn near impossible to keep anything quiet in the wrestling business.

Curt tried everything to stay alive but, with his local TV company dropping him from their programing, it was only a matter of time before his wrestling business collapsed.

Geraldine placed her chicken dish in the middle of the table and stood back to judge its perfection. She pushed some peas atop the mound of pinkish meat and hard vegetation and seemed finally pleased. Both men awaited her go-ahead.

"Now, dig in," she said, beaming with pride. "To the meal I mean."

Curt, well trained around his mother's cooking, avoided the meat altogether but he happily watched Shane dig into the undercooked bird.

Geraldine's phone rang and Curt hopped up nervously from his sitting position. "I'll get it," he said, knocking over his drink and toppling his chair in his stampede to get to the phone first.

"Jesus, Curtis," Geraldine replied. "Do you have to be a fat fucking elephant?"

Curt picked up the receiver and walked its long cord into the living room.

"Hello?" Curt said, half whispering.

"Is this Curt?" Danno asked.

Curt could hardly contain the relief in his voice. "Danno?"

"Yeah," Danno answered from his office in New York. "It's me. I got your message."

"Do we have a deal?" Curt asked quickly.

Danno was surprised at Curt's forwardness but, after struggling with his dying business for over a year, Curt was in no position to be coy.

"Yeah, we got a deal. But this is between us. If I hear for a second that the word is out on this deal, then I pull my offer and spend my time blacklisting you," Danno said.

Curt wondered whether Danno meant he would blacklist him even more.

"I just want out. Going out of business is an expensive thing," Curt said, looking directly at Shane Montrose.

"I'll buy your territory Curt."

Curt held the phone into his palm so Danno couldn't hear him for a second. "Thank you Jesus," he whispered before re-engaging in the conversation.

"Okay," Danno continued. "Are you going to be in Grobie's for a while? I have to run some things past Troy and make sure this can all be squared in Lawyerland."

"This line isn't great," Curt lied. "I got the number of the payphone down the street. You should ring me back there instead."

Curt turned to see if Shane could hear the conversation. Shane was watching from the table but couldn't hear anything. He gave

Curt the 'do-we-have-a-deal?' look.

Curt quickly summoned his depressed and deflated face as he shook his head in reply. "No deal," he silently mouthed.

Shane watched Curt turn his back to him and continue to talk into the phone. He noticed Curt's clenched fist open as he slid his hand into his pocket.

Nobody puts their hand in their pocket when they get bad news.

Grobie pushed Shane's plate closer to him.

"Eat up," she said. "A body like that can't run on empty."

Shane rose quietly from the table and walked towards Curt.

"You don't mind if I watch you leave?" Grobie asked.

Shane didn't answer. He was too busy trying to figure out if he was getting cut out of his deal. Too busy trying to calculate whether yet another promoter was trying to fuck him over. He needed his cut more than any other time in his life.

Curt heard the footsteps move closer and he hung up and steadied himself before turning around.

"He wasn't interested. Not yet. He said no but I think he's just taking time to weigh this all up. Maybe in six months or something like that."

Shane could only nod. The more Curt talked the more he could feel him lying. After years of watching various owners fuck him around, he had developed a pretty good bullshit meter.

"Do we have wine?" Curt asked his mother, already knowing the answer.

Grobie, still at the table, shook her head. Wine was for queers. Grobie Magee's house was full of vodka, whiskey and a little something her uncle made her drink.

Curt grabbed his jacket and keys and left.

Ten minutes later Shane was fucking Grobie on her bathroom floor. Like most Rats Shane had sex with over the years, Grobie didn't seem to be *into it*. It was like she was somewhere else. It was only when he'd stop and try and catch her eye that she'd snap to and moan a little.

The bathroom door was slightly open. At first Shane was worried about Curt coming back and seeing them. Now he was worried that Curt would come back and not see them.

So Shane Montrose scuttled back just far enough to poke the bathroom door open further.

He was sick of promoters looking at him as dull-witted. They saw the wrestlers as dullards – a necessary evil in the attraction business. There was no way Curt was going to tell him about Danno's call. He knew there was no way he was going to get a straight story from Curt or Danno.

But if Curt wouldn't talk to him and Danno wouldn't talk to him, maybe another Garland would.

Five months before the murder.

New Jersey.

Shane lay naked with Annie Garland. The dingy room was small, and sweaty. Far from what they were both used to. Shane usually liked to pay for a higher-class joint, but he was now counting coins and actively avoiding people who were looking for their money back.

Things with Curt were bad. And he smelled a rat.

They both lay silently and Annie wasn't even all that sure that she liked the man beside her. She wanted to blame him, all by himself, for making her do these things. These backhanded things that made her sick to her stomach.

But, in truth she knew that Shane didn't do anything more than make the call. She took it, entertained it and followed him.

It was her. And her alone she hated. But she had a way of making most of that hatred disappear. Certainly for a while anyway.

"I wish you never gave me one of these in the first place," Annie said as she inspected the small pill between her fingers.

Shane grabbed it and threw it into his own smoke-filled mouth.

"I did you a favor," he said as he blew a stream of smoke towards a ceiling that had obviously seen a lot of smoke in its day.

Annie rolled onto her side and reached into her bag where there were plenty more pills waiting. They were organized, in a civil manner, in a nice embossed silver box. She thought it added a little class to a totally classless pursuit.

That little metal tomb held Annie Garland totally and completely.

"Those little things help me do what I do," Shane said of the pills. "They let me go another week and then another year. They let me earn money. They let me walk around."

Annie carefully placed one in her mouth, all ladylike, and swallowed it down with a waiting drink of water.

"Me too," she said.

"I got two bum knees, a ripped up shoulder and the pain in my back sometimes makes me think of killing myself. What have you got, lady?"

"There's different kinds of pain," she simply answered.

Shane stubbed out his cigarette and turned to Annie, resting his head in the palm of his hand.

"What pain does a woman like you have?" he asked disbelievingly.

Annie could feel the warm washing comfort of her previous intake start to surround her shoulders and work its way up along the back of her head.

"None," she answered. "I've got nothing to worry about."

Shane looked her up and down – something her husband would never do. To Annie, Shane was rougher, more base, more simple. Over the years it despised her that she was attracted to him. That he was two steps away from being an animal. No tact, no manners, no plans, no strategy. Just all instinct, grabbing and aggression.

But he looked at her. Like her husband never would.

She imagined herself being with him. Not having to worry about him and his supper and how his clothes looked and what his mood was. She wouldn't have to rear him and prop him up and make sure she placed his keys in the very same fucking place every single morning of their marriage because if they were two inches from that place she would have to come down the stairs and place them in his fat fucking hand.

She was lying beside a man who could and did look after himself. She knew he was the type of man who lied and fucked dubious women and paid more attention to what he looked like than what his woman looked like. He was attracted to shiny things and dangerous things and things that could harm him.

And she thought she loved that. She just wasn't sure. What she did know was that she was tired of fighting it. Tired of wondering. Tired of trying to remember what it was like to be with a man who wanted her. Who at least acted like he loved her. A man with some fight in him. A man who wasn't ready to coast to the end.

She was older and softer in places. But she wasn't ready to be locked in the big house and put herself on pause until Danno came home.

"What are you thinking about?" he asked as he rubbed his hand around her ribcage and under her breast.

"I'm thinking about my husband," she said as she swallowed another pill.

"Maybe you should take it easy on those."

Annie lay back and waited to forget. Or not care. Hopefully both, but more than likely the latter.

"Word is he's doing something with Curt?" Shane asked, hoping to sound more chatty than snoopy.

"Who?"

"Danno."

Annie grabbed his hand and threw it from her body. "Do you think I want you talking about my husband while you feel me up?"

"You brought him up."

Annie wanted to get up and get dressed. Then she didn't want to get up and do anything.

"He'd have me killed if he knew, wouldn't he?" Shane asked in a more somber voice.

"Yes," she said without hesitation. "And me too."

"I wouldn't let anything happen to you," he said.

"You wouldn't have any choice."

"Yeah, well, if anything bad happens to you and I find whoever did it, I'll kill them where they stand."

Annie turned her head and smiled at Shane's sentiment.

"I'm not joking," he said.

"I know."

There was a slight pause where they both weighed up the outcome of their meetings ever getting out.

"I don't want to talk about Danno here," Annie said.

Shane could see his door closing, his opportunity fading. He needed to find out if Curt was telling the truth when he said that Danno wasn't doing a deal. For Shane Montrose, Curt selling to Danno meant there was enough money for Shane to finally get *his* money.

"He doesn't tell me anything," Annie said, now more relaxed about everything.

"He's never said anything about Curt Magee or Texas?" Shane asked.

"What? I don't know," she answered as she began to melt more into herself.

Shane didn't believe her. He didn't believe her at all. He started to get the gnawing feeling that everyone was about to make a lot of money. Except him.

And not making money was an unacceptable situation for Shane Montrose. He had spent a lot of money on the promise of his slice coming through. And he knew his bankers weren't the suit wearing kind.

Five days after the murder.

New York.

Shane took in the grounds and the stables but he didn't notice any cars in the drive. Danno's house was huge and square and it stood still in the morning quiet outside.

He wasn't sure if this was a good idea as the cab crept slowly up the long driveway. Maybe Danno wasn't here? Maybe there were fifty cars parked around the back. Who knew?

He paid the taxi driver from a slab of folded notes. He tipped him a fifty and signed his autograph on a copy of the daily paper.

The headline read:

SENATOR TENENBAUM HOME AND RESTING.

"Thank you. I saw you wrestle in The Garden many times over the years," the cab driver excitedly told his famous passenger.

Shane nodded politely and stood small under the shadow of the house. He walked cautiously towards the steps as his ride pulled off down the driveway.

His breath was stale from drink — but that wasn't anything unusual. His face was rough and his clothes were the same as the day before. He survived Danno and the wake. Literally. Now he wanted to find out where Curt Magee was hiding. With the bounty Danno had out, Shane knew it was only a matter of time before Danno found out first.

And Danno wasn't the only one who loved her at one time.

Shane took the first, large step towards the house. The air smelt different after the rain in this part of New York. It was fresh and subtle.

Shane took another step whilst looking around. Danno swung open his front door and marched with intent towards his visitor. "What the fuck do you want with me?"

"I ... ," Shane struggled to piece together a sentence that would make sense.

Danno took out his gun and jammed it against the forehead of the wrestler in front of him. It wasn't the same gun that lay on Danno's bed with Danno's suit. This was a different gun, meant for other people.

"Danno, please," Shane begged. "Let me ... "

"What?"

"Let me ... "

"Let you what?" Danno said as he grabbed the back of Shane's head and bore the barrel of his gun in deeper.

"I just ... "

"You just what? Speak. You fucking tell me why you're at my door. Tell me why I shouldn't blow your fucking head off on these steps?"

Danno could see it. He didn't want to acknowledge it, but he could see it. Shane Montrose was lost too.

"I'm sorry," Shane simply said.

"You keep saying that. What do you want me to say to you?" Danno tried to raise the same level of anger that he had a sentence ago, but couldn't. He whipped the gun barrel away from Shane's head.

"Don't make me kill you," Danno warned as he turned back towards his house. He began to tremble from adrenaline. This wasn't him. He would run from conflict a month ago. He was getting too old to be suspicious of everyone. It was wearing him down. He wanted to rip that weight from his stomach. That deadness that lay in there and twisted back and forth. That gnawing instinct to lay down and stay there.

"Danno?"

Danno stopped.

"I want to help you," Shane said. "You don't need to get involved in this. I'd happily ... tell me where Curt Magee is ... "

Danno looked Shane dead in the eye, grabbed him by the jaw bone, and discharged a shot downward into his foot.

The pain and shock took a split second to register – but when it did, Shane collapsed, screaming in agony.

"You shot me. You fucking shot me," he roared in disbelief.

"For years I watched her leaving this house and I wondered where she was going. The next time I see you," Danno calmly said as he pointed his gun at Shane's head, "I won't aim any lower than your face."

Shane covered up. Danno stood over him long enough to

punctuate his dominance. He saw the broken flesh exposed through the disintegrated designer shoe and the blood beginning to gush from Shane's mangled foot.

"Now get the fuck out of here," Danno warned as he re-entered his home and slammed the door.

Danno already knew where Curt was. He didn't need anyone else's help to find him anymore. But he thought he needed someone else's help in killing him.

CHAPTER TEN

Madison Square Garden was the mecca. It was the spiritual home of the Garland's wrestling company. Danno's father ran there for years before Danno took over and did the same. Every month they would finish their traveling loop in the sold-out Garden.

Every month except this one. Tickets for this one were slow to say the least.

Ricky walked through the hushed backstage entrance on the ground floor. His shoes tapped along the concrete floor past the rubbish stacked high against the cold brick walls. Above his head a confusion of cables and pipes ran exposed in all directions.

The crew had been in all day setting up and getting ready. There were wrestlers from all over the country above his head. And a whole lot of problems too.

Ricky followed the corridor around to the right and saw a couple of forklift trucks drizzled with arena-hands taking a smoke break. Ricky nodded in their direction and walked up the ramp, tapping his hand off the battered railing.

He took a sharp right and passed a train of pallets, still packed and waiting to be opened. The snugly wrapped silver piping followed him along the ceiling and large hanging lights lit the way. It was more like a boiler room than the most famous arena in the world.

Another right turn brought him into the jaws of the large service elevator with the worn down floor. In it, Ricky felt small and insignificant. He knew that his time in the large box was probably going to be the only quiet time of the next few days. He pushed the button and the protective cage slid down across the opening. Two metal doors then engulfed the cage like a closing mouth and the floor began to shudder under his feet. The short journey to the backstage area began. This was going to be a hard day, with hard decisions to be made.

All without Danno.

The elevator came to a stop and the doors slid back into hiding. It was noisier now. The backstage area had the hum of people behind doors, laughing in distant hallways. Ricky steadied himself and walked from the elevator through the same double doors he had passed countless times before. He bypassed all of the open and half open doorways and walked directly down to the opening that led onto the arena floor.

"Ricky?" Danno called from a half-opened door.

Ricky stopped dead. Danno's voice was the last he expected to hear, but was the one he hoped he would.

He backtracked and peered around the door.

"I think I've found him," Danno said.

"Curt?" Ricky whispered trying to drag Danno's volume down a few notches.

Danno nodded. He was distant and distracted.

"How?"

"We have to go," Danno said as he passed Ricky in the doorway. "I have a cab waiting."

Ricky stayed still on his feet as Danno walked off.

"Boss?" Ricky said.

Both men were standing inside Madison Square Garden. It was a few hours away from bell time and only one of them had wrestling or business anywhere near being on their mind.

"I can't," Ricky said.

Danno walked back and looked Ricky in the face. "I said I found him."

Ricky was a loyal soldier — but he knew wrestling was wrestling and business was business. What Danno wanted him to get involved in was something completely different. Something he decided that he didn't want any hand, act or part in.

"I don't have time for this," Danno said. "They might have someone talking in there."

"Who might have someone talking?" Ricky asked.

"The cops. I got word that someone has turned and is going to rat us out."

Ricky hardly even knew how to form the small word stuck in his throat. "What?" he finally managed.

Danno turned. "I'll fill you in on the way."

"On the way where?"

Ricky marched after Danno and gently grabbed his swinging arm. "I'm staying here," he said with his head bowed. "Unless you tell me that you don't want me here. But that thing you're leaving to do right now. I understand. But... "

"But what?"

"That's not ... I've got ... " Ricky pointed down to the opening that led out onto the famous arena floor. "*That's* what I signed up for. With your father before you. And with you."

Danno turned square on to his right-hand man. "You're pulling out of this thing?"

Ricky very reluctantly nodded. "Yeah."

"Are you sure?"

Ricky nodded again.

"Well then, you're a fucking faggot," Danno said as he slapped Ricky across the face.

Ricky immediately filled with anger. The outcome of years of trust and hard work and sacrifice in front of them both and it was down to this – an insult with his hand and an insult with his mouth.

"I'm trying to understand," Ricky said. "I'm trying to imagine what it's like to be in your shoes. But if you ever raise your hand to me again you better have an ambulance waiting and not a cab."

Danno stood in front of him defiantly.

Ricky continued. "And if you don't stop this path you're on, you're going to pull everything down with you. Your life *and* my life."

Ricky wanted him to stay. He wanted Danno to honor the business. The thing that was still alive and they could do something about. The thing his father built before him and the thing that was handed to him as a gift. A near hundred-year-old gift.

Danno turned away and walked for his cab. He didn't want to go either. But he felt that he had to live up to his promise. Even if it meant changing who he was.

If Ricky wasn't willing to help then Danno needed to make contact with a man who would.

The city had already made the white bandages stained and dirty. Shane Montrose dragged himself up the stairs of his shitty hotel. Every step was a cruel and painful heave. There was a lump missing from the side of his foot and apparently several of the smaller bones were broken from the sheer velocity of the shot.

It was hard to tell the full extent of the damage without getting an x-ray – and it was hard to get one of those without going to a hospital. He knew he didn't have time for that.

There was a doctor Upstate who was very friendly with professional wrestlers. Every town had such a doctor. Someone who liked big cash money for a 'call-out' and access to his prescriptions book.

But even the shady doctor warned him of the dangers of not going to an emergency room. Shane instead left with a clean wound, a tight dressing and a pocketful of sedatives, barbiturates and a little bag of powder completely off the books.

All he wanted to do was to get to Curt Magee.

He unlocked his door, triple locked it from the inside, and staggered back onto his noisy sprung bed.

The pain was excruciating.

He thought in all his years of wrestling, and all the injuries that such a life brings, that he developed a significant pain threshold.

Maybe the only thing that kept him moving was that threshold.

He rattled around in his pocket looking for the pills. For the first time in his adult life he was calculating on how *not* to get too stoned. Even in intense pain he had to keep his wits about him.

He threw his arm out and slapped around the bedside locker, looking for his watch. In doing so, it slid like a snake onto the floor.

"Fuck. You. Fuck … "

The rough sound of his phone ringing startled him into jolting his own foot. It took him a couple of seconds to digest that his phone was ringing.

His phone was ringing.

Shane grabbed the phone. "Hello?"

"Shane?" the scared sounding voice asked.

It was Curt Magee.

Shane moaned in discomfort as he pulled a gun from his drawer and checked the chamber.

"Tell me where you are," Shane said in his most faux sympathetic voice.

Danno felt the neglected roads underneath him and heard the blaring of the car horns in front of him. His checkered taxi's windshield wipers were doing all they could to beat away an open New York sky.

The 8772 bus pulled into traffic and chugged out a cloud of black smoke as it struggled to keep up.

On the backseat with him was a discarded newspaper that read:

FBI Finds Nixon Aides Sabotaged Democrats.

The whole country was working each other. Power grabbing from the top all the way down. He wished it was still that simple for him. For a split second he forgot the stomach churning events of the last few days and remembered a time when his business was all about the pieces on the board. He loved to move them around, look for the openings and make his move.

Danno Garland wasn't a killer. Or, at least he wasn't born one. But he knew he would have to be one at least once more before his own judgment happened.

He got out of the cab, overpaid the grateful cab driver and walked into the park. Around him people scurried for his vacated ride, shielding themselves from the rain with anything they could put above their heads. Jackets, newspapers and umbrellas.

Danno didn't notice the weather or didn't care.

Across the street Nestor Chapman sat in his unmarked car watching Danno.

"Any sign?" asked a voice over his radio system.

Nestor picked up the phone-shaped receiver and placed it to his lips, but didn't answer.

"Are you there, copy?" the voice asked again.

Nestor again didn't answer. He reluctantly put the receiver down and opened his car door.

Danno walked the pathway and scanned passers-by to see if they were his contact.

"Danno," Mickey Jack Crisp said from a park bench.

Danno recognized the frame. The outline of his hair. His long, thick sideburns. Danno immediately knew that he was looking at the man who buried Proctor after he put a bullet in his head.

And that was who he was looking for.

Danno had only seen Mickey in the dark field a couple of nights previously when he held Proctor King on his knees.

"Are you Mickey?" Danno asked before approaching.

Mickey nodded. He seemed totally at ease with the torrential rain hopping off the bench under him.

Danno walked closer. "I want you to help me kill this man."

Danno passed Mickey an oversized envelope from his coat with Curt's details and a stack of cash in it. "I just need you to bring him to me. And I'll do the rest. I have a chartered plane. It's all in there. Let's go."

"Now?" Mickey asked.

"Yes. Now. You got a problem with that?"

Mickey seemed torn. "I can meet you in a couple of hours. I just have to finish something first."

Danno looked at him suspiciously. "It's now or I go and get

someone else."

Mickey's mouth was full of questions but Danno just walked on.

Nestor watched from a distance.

Mickey drove the beaten up brown Plymouth into the rain. Danno was silent beside him. He noticed Mickey's shoes were mucky and the floor of the car was the same.

"Rain destroys everything," Mickey said.

Danno wasn't so sure.

"What's the smell?" Danno asked.

Mickey decided to elaborate. "I don't have anywhere to stay up here. I was just supposed to come to town and do… " Mickey didn't finish the sentence. He knew Danno knew what he meant. He was supposed to come to New York and kill Proctor King. "And then I was supposed to head back to Florida … "

"Florida?" Danno asked.

Mickey nodded. "Some other things came up so I hung around. Bottom line is I slept in the car."

Danno knew somewhere in the back of his head that Mickey was from Florida. He just forgot.

He thought about the note that was left under his door.

There's a heatwave coming up from Florida. Make sure and cover up.

He looked back as far as his fat body would let him to see if they were being followed. Mickey could sense his sudden jumpiness.

"You doing okay, man?" he asked.

"Yeah," Danno said as he adjusted all the mirrors to let him see the angles from behind.

Now Mickey was getting jumpy too. "Is there something happening here that I should be aware of?"

Danno shook his head. Unconvincingly.

"You need to tell me what's going on here or I'm turning this car the fuck around Danno," Mickey said.

Danno thought about where to start and what Mickey needed to know.

"They're tailing us."

"Who is?"

"The cops," Danno answered.

Now Mickey started to panic. "Why are they tailing us?"

"When we get to the airport, you drop me off at the terminal and go and park. I have a plane waiting for us," Danno said as he took back Mickey's envelope and wrote out the hangar number on the front of it.

"And then what?"

"You drop me off, park the car and meet me there. If you get there and I don't, I still want you to go do what we've discussed. Only difference is, I want you to hold him there, alive. I'll make my way to you when the time is right."

Mickey was about to argue all the legitimate issues that would raise.

"I'll give you an extra hundred grand. And tell Little Terry the same. Hundred each."

"Who's Little Terry?"

"My pilot."

Mickey could hear in Danno's voice that Danno wanted to do the dirty end of Mickey's job for him, again.

"If we get split up, my house phone number is in the information I gave you," Danno said.

"Deal," Mickey said as he put out his hand. Danno obliged. Mickey's firm response gave him some hope.

"But don't let the cops look through this car," Mickey said.

Danno nodded. Mickey made sure to look Danno in the face so Danno would understand how serious he was.

"There's a couple of things in this car that could get us both in some trouble."

One week before the murder.

Texas.

Tat-tat-tat on the window. But there was no answer. The large waiting man tried again. Tat-tat-tat. Nothing. He checked his watch and took a couple of steps back to look up at the top windows.

He was outside a nice house. Big, but not huge. Certainly owned by wealthy people though. It was freshly painted with colorful flowers in the window boxes outside.

"Hello?" the visitor called. "Hello?"

He walked around the side of the house and cupped the ground floor window. It was quiet inside. No signs of life. The place was well kept and orderly.

"Hello?"

He could see through to the kitchen. It certainly seemed empty.

Crystal Montrose held her breath in the broom closet of her kitchen. She didn't have time to warn her five year old daughter to be quiet and she could hear her little footsteps on the stairs.

"Mommy," she called.

The little girl was frightened by the sudden quietness downstairs. She knew her mother was usually singing, watching loud TV or talking up a storm on the telephone.

"Mom?" she said as she warily looked into the kitchen.

Crystal couldn't move with fear. She tried to 'shh' her daughter but she knew her voice was too low to matter.

"Mommy?"

She could hear her little girl's voice begin to tremble. Crystal prayed that the man outside was gone.

The scared little girl walked into the kitchen doorway and saw her mother, with tear stains on her cheeks and her finger to her lips, direct her back up the stairs.

But it was too late.

The back door burst open with a terrifying crack as the intruder kicked the door in. The little girl screamed and ran frantically up the stairs. Crystal tried to follow her but she was pulled back by her intruder who had two handfuls of her hair.

"Where is he?" the man shouted.

"I don't know," she screamed as she tried in vain to fight back.

"You tell him that if I don't see him within seven days that I'm going to find you and set you alight."

Crystal turned away in terror and the man let her go. She ran upstairs to try and protect her little girl.

"He has one week to get me my money," the man said calmly from the kitchen before he left.

His throat was raw from too much smoking and his hands were shaky from too much coke. Shane Montrose was coming back home after two weeks on the road.

And Texas was a huge, awkward state to travel by car. He'd been to Houston, Fort Worth, Dallas, San Antonio and Austin. Twice. He would now come off the road for a day or two and then hit some smaller 'spot' towns in between the loop of *Houston, Forth Worth, Dallas, San Antonio and Austin. Twice.* He had the names of the towns and cities playing around in his head like a continuous record.

He was getting too old to be struggling with a state so huge. Most of his colleagues were trying to get to San Francisco. Small trips, great weather and home every night.

Shane Montrose was a star. But he was a regional star. The guy with the heavyweight title was the national star. Flown everywhere, driven the rest. Best of hotels, more women than he could handle and the biggest money – by far – at the end of the night.

On drives like this one being home every night sounded great to him. But he knew he'd be bored in a week and would be out partying and chasing tail.

That's the reason he was coming home to wife number three.

About five minutes away from home he saw a man walking in the middle of the road waving his arms. Shane checked the rearview mirror and saw that his was the only car on the road. The dark, secondary road.

Fuck it. He floored it and headed straight for the wandering man. The last couple of years had all been about surviving, avoiding lenders and making it to the next day.

Curt was only paying him a percentage of the gate in every town, "until Danno comes to his senses."

The more speed he picked up, the closer he got, the more the man in the road looked terrified.

"Hey," the man in the road shouted.

"Bert?" Shane wondered to himself.

Shane and Bert sat silently as they pulled into Bert's house. Shane had been filled in on what happened earlier. He didn't know what to say.

Crystal sat out on the porch and waited for Shane to arrive. She was smoking – he'd never seen her do that.

"Where's the little one?" Shane asked as he approached.

Crystal stood and walked into his pathway. "She's asleep. Finally."

Bert entered the house and left them to it.

"I'm going to make this simple, Shane. I don't know what you do on the road. I can guess, I can imagine, but I don't want to know. But when your actions send a man to our home to do us harm, and he was serious, I don't know what to do anymore."

Shane put out his arms for a hug. "Baby, I'm sorry."

Crystal began to cry. "I couldn't even call the cops because I don't know if you're involved in something illegal or not. I don't know what to do to protect my child."

Shane put his hand at the back of her head and tried to coax her in closer to him. She pushed him away.

"You go back out there and fix whatever it is you've dragged us all into. Do you hear me? You moved us again with promises of a mansion and cars and vacations every other month. Where is it? Where's the deal you made? I bet everyone else is making more than you. As usual there's a pot of money somewhere and everyone else is dipping in to it except my husband. Mister fucking Big Time. The one the whole business is laughing at. Again. Open your eyes. You're a joke."

Crystal walked into her brother's house.

Matthew Miller strode along Old Slip late and smoking. He knew the second part of his day was only starting even though he could feel the dark evening coming on.

On the opposite side of the street he could see his building, long and narrow, almost make its way down to the East River. No one in his department knew yet that the coming Christmas would be their last in that building.

He was just waiting on word to see if his First precinct was, in fact, going to be amalgamated with the Fourth. If that was the case then his building wasn't big enough to hold both crews. They'd certainly have to move.

"Captain Miller?" called a voice from behind.

Miller stopped and turned. He knew the voice but didn't know from where. He saw a man hurry to catch up. It was Dr. Melvin Pritchard, head of the New York Athletic State Commission, the governing body for both boxing and wrestling in New York. Amateur wrestling he could handle, but *professional* wrestling made him sick.

"Sir," called Melvin. "My name is Dr. Melvin Pritchard. I believe we spoke on the phone."

Miller nodded and extended his hand. "How do you do Doctor. I'm in a hurry I'm afraid."

Miller continued towards his building. Melvin followed. He wanted to make sure that Danno Garland didn't slip the cops like he did him and his organization. Melvin had spent a lot of his time trying to get professional wrestling, and Danno Garland, put under the federal spotlight.

"I was wondering how your investigation is going? With regard to Senator Tenenbaum?"

"I can't comment."

Both men dodged the oncoming crowds.

"And Danno Garland?" Melvin asked.

The captain stopped.

134

"I can't comment on him either. Look, I appreciate the information you gave us over the phone, I really do, but the senator is saying he didn't see anything that can help us."

"Do you know where Danno was the night the senator was attacked?" Melvin asked.

Miller could see the lamps at either side of the precinct door glow a couple of hundred feet away. He wanted to keep walking but he was sure he was going to have to hear Melvin talk one way or the other.

"No. I don't know where he was," he answered.

"He was with me," Melvin said with a pause. "He called to meet me in JFK that night and the night before. He sat in front of me and said nothing. As a matter of fact he did nothing for hours. He just watched the clock."

Miller was failing to see how this was implicating Danno in any way.

"He used me as an alibi. He made me recite the date and the time before he stood up and left. That was the night the senator got attacked."

Miller was unimpressed. "It means nothing. We'll keep looking. I can promise you that."

He turned from Melvin and took off into his stride again.

"Sir," Melvin called.

Miller was short on patience.

"Sir, indeed," Miller replied. "This fucking city is choking. The Bronx is burning, we don't have the money to pay for our schools. I'm hearing about German Shepherds being posted down in the subway. Right here, where you're standing, we had to bag up three Chinks who welched on a fucking bet last week." Miller could see he had Melvin's attention. "I don't give a fuck about what you think a bunch of conmen are doing to the spirit of competition."

Captain Miller again began to walk but Melvin stayed put.

"Did you know his wife was murdered?" Melvin asked as Miller walked away.

Melvin's parting words stopped Miller in his tracks. He turned and made his way back to the doctor against the flow of foot traffic.

"What?" the captain asked.

"I still have to oversee these people as head of the Athletic Commission. I hear things when I'm with them. There's something going on. Danno's wife was killed in Texas a couple of days ago," Melvin said.

Miller seemed genuinely taken aback.

"She was murdered?"

Melvin nodded. He could see he now had the captain's attention.

"We were trying to shut Danno's business down. The senator and I. We were one day away from getting the ball rolling when the senator was attacked. Or he was made an example of, I should say. A week or so later, Danno's wife turns up dead in a hotel in Texas. I don't know how one thing links the other. And maybe they don't. But I thought you should know."

The captain took a second to digest what Melvin was saying.

Melvin continued, "I don't know *what's* happening, but *something* is happening. Something is going down and they're starting to get sloppy."

Captain Miller needed to know what that was. He thanked Melvin and left him on the sidewalk. He needed to find out what was going on. He needed to find out where Nestor Chapman was.

The backstage area was packed with wrestlers stretching and going through their matches. New faces from all over the country. Ricky had the book in his hand with all the matches listed out.

"Where's Ginny?" Ricky asked someone from the ring crew.

He was pointed towards the arena floor. Ricky should have known. He marched through the short tunnel and could see Ginny in the ring with a couple of other people. The further along the floor he got the more he could see a small audience of wrestlers in the stands.

Ginny was on all fours and was talking to Oscar Dewsbury who was standing behind him. The same Oscar that Ricky grabbed by the throat the day before.

Ginny couldn't see that Oscar was pretending to fuck him from behind. Oscar was miming and mugging for the onlookers and pretending to slap Ginny in the back of his head.

The other person in the ring was a stranger to Ricky. A stranger who was trying to hold in his laughter at the degrading scene in front of him.

Ginny spoke to the visitor, "So when you get scooped up for a slam you tuck your chin in and make sure that your feet come down to protect your kidneys. The more points that hit the mat the better."

"What's going on?" Ricky asked as he approached the ring and jumped up onto the apron.

Oscar immediately jumped up and dropped his head in feigned respect.

"Who's this?" Ricky wanted to know of the stranger in the ring.

The small audience of wrestlers in the stands upped and left quickly. Ricky parted the ring ropes and entered the ring.

"That's ... I forget his name. He's an All-American from the State of Michigan," Ginny said about the visitor. "He wants to get into the business."

"Is that right?" Ricky asked as he approached Oscar in the ring.

"He's my cousin," Oscar answered without looking up. He knew that Ricky saw what he was doing behind Ginny's back. "He wants to try out... "

"And you let him in this ring?" Ricky asked.

"You said it was okay," Ginny intervened.

Ricky knew that Oscar had filled Ginny full of bullshit. "I said it was okay?" Ricky asked Oscar.

Oscar was getting nervous at Ricky's questioning. "No, Mr ... "

Ricky stopped him mid-sentence with a short right hand that knocked him out clean.

"Hey, hey," Ginny said as he used the ropes to get himself off the mat.

Ricky put his hand up to keep Ginny at arms length. He wasn't done yet.

He next went over to the outsider. The one who was laughing. The one he'd never even seen before.

"You see, the thing you must have in this business is respect," he said. "Respect earns you the right to stand in this ring."

Ricky unzipped his jacket and threw it over the top rope. "What's your name?"

"Franklin," the All-American answered.

He was stocky with a huge neck and cauliflower ears from years of grappling.

Ricky pulled the young man into his face. "What we do in this ring is no fucking joke."

The amateur wrestler gripped Ricky's wrists but he couldn't stop Ricky from hoisting him into the air and dropping him hard on his neck and head, folding him up like an accordion.

Franklin's sporting pride made him stumble to his feet – but he was clearly stunned and in pain.

"Men have broken their backs to be in this ring in this arena,"

Ricky said as he grabbed Franklin and slid his arm under his chin and began to choke him. "So you don't fucking belong here."

Franklin began to turn a shade of purple and the veins in his eyes began to break with the pressure of the hold. Ginny quietly tried to loosen the hold by putting himself between Ricky and the All-American.

"C'mon. It's only this fake stuff that you hear about. Not like what you do, hah?" Ricky asked the flailing young man in his clench.

Ricky released the choke and Franklin flopped to the mat without any control.

"What are you doing Ricky?" Ginny shouted.

"They're mocking you," Ricky said as he walked to the ropes to see what damage he had done.

"I was showing them the basics. That's what they pay me to do," Ginny answered.

"No one pays you," Ricky said.

Ricky dropped to the mat and rolled outside. He grabbed Franklin's arm and dragged him out of the ring and dropped him on the floor.

"Someone get this piece of shit out of this building," Ricky shouted towards the wrestlers in the back.

"And tell him," Ricky said to Ginny about Oscar, "he's fired when he wakes up."

Ricky left the ringside area and was ready for the event that night.

Fucking show time.

CHAPTER ELEVEN

Five days after the murder.

New York.

Danno walked silently towards the sharp-nosed white plane. He felt like he was only hours away from making good on the promise to his wife.

He had gotten Curt's whereabouts from Tanner Blackwell. It was in exchange for the bounty - and one of the heavyweight titles. An honor that Danno would have never given Tanner on a normal day. But there was nothing normal about this day.

Curt had hit the road and was gone when everyone was out looking for him. Over the last day or two he snuck back to his mother's house for some money and supplies. Grobie couldn't help but whine about her son's return to some rookie who was going down on her outside a bar.

And nothing travels faster in the wrestling world than some juicy gossip wrapped up in a story about fucking.

Curt was at Grobie's, but he wasn't going to stay there long. Danno knew he didn't have much time.

"Sir?" called a uniformed police officer as he approached Danno. Both he and his partner where acting a little wary as they got closer.

"Sir," the officer continued. "Are you Danno Garland?"

"Why?" Danno asked.

In the distance he could see the steps of his plane still connected and waiting for him.

"Answer the question, sir."

Danno knew time was running out. He needed to get to Curt Magee before he disappeared again.

He should have been more worried about Shane Montrose getting there first.

"Sir," came a way more impatient voice.

Danno conceded. "Yes. I'm Danno Garland. What's the problem?"

One of the police officers stepped forward. "You have to come with us, sir."

"What's this all about?" Danno demanded to know.

They had nothing concrete but that didn't stop them from impeding his travel with questioning and anything else they could think of to make his life harder. Captain Miller didn't trust Danno to leave and not come back. All he could do was get his men to stall him.

Danno turned around and saw his plane door closing.

"Come with us, sir."

Five days after the murder.

New York.

The most flamboyant strut in all of professional wrestling was unrecognizable. Shane Montrose limped and grimaced and dragged his loosely bandaged foot. He held the walls of JFK International as he walked, foot to heel, across its crowded floor.

He made it to the American Airlines desk with the relief of the last stroke of a drowning man. "Dallas," he said to the perfectly polished woman at the desk as he tried to control the sound of pain leaving his mouth.

"Are you okay sir?" the middle-aged woman asked.

Shane slammed a mixed ball of cash onto the counter and nodded. He was trembling and sweaty.

"Sir?" she asked again with a concerned voice. "Is everything alright?"

Shane deflected, "Can you just get me a ticket?"

"One moment, please," she said as she rose from her position and looked around the terminal.

Shane pushed himself away from the counter. "I'll just be a second."

The eyes of the American Airlines worker scoured the room more frantically. "I just want to get you some help sir."

Shane mumbled about 'washing up' and painfully scurried towards the restroom.

Inside he locked himself in a small vacant cubicle and sat on the toilet seat. His foot was unmercifully throbbing as he lifted it from the wet floor and lay it across his opposite thigh.

He rested his clammy forehead against the cubicle wall and openly cried in pain. It was wearing on him and he didn't know how much longer he could avoid the lure of the strong sedatives in his pocket.

At this rate he wasn't going to make it onto the flight. He looked too suspicious and he was drawing attention to himself.

Shane removed the gun from his jacket and wrapped it time and again in toilet paper until it was covered completely and made indistinguishable as a shape. What was he thinking bringing that into an airport?

He steadied himself and exited the cubicle into the empty restroom. He dropped his gun in the trash can before walking again to the desk where he found the same lady.

"Sir?"

"I'm sorry," Shane said, immediately cutting her off. "It's been a hell of a day."

He read her name tag.

"Neve."

The woman stood and looked over the counter at the disheveled man in front of her. He was pasty, and gaunt, and sweaty and his clothes were creased and unwashed. He had a giant, dirty bandage around his foot and he struggled to stand.

"That's a nice name. Neve."

She was unimpressed.

"I *have to* get to Texas, ma'am."

"And why is that?"

"You want the truth?"

"Yes sir, I do."

Shane gingerly took a step forward. "Because I just left my nephew in county morgue about an hour ago. And now I have to go and tell my bother that his son is dead."

Shane pressed down on his own injured foot, which quickly brought pain to his face and tears to his eyes. "The little boy was with me. And we crashed. And all I got was this," he said nodding to his foot. "And he … "

Shane could see the counter lady beginning to melt.

"And I *have to* tell my brother face to face. I *have to* do that. Even if it means going like this. Now can you help me?"

"Hello?" Lenny half-heartedly shouted around the side of Mrs. Dumont's house. Even though he grew up next door, Lenny hadn't been on her property since he was a child. And with good reason. He could never really look her in the eye since the time she whooped him right outside her house because his left ball was hanging out as he ran up and down outside her house. Lenny made his pals laugh. Mrs. Dumont made Lenny cry shortly thereafter.

"Mrs. Dumont?" he said again gently.

Lenny had no choice but to talk to her. She had the key to his mother's house.

Lenny opened the door and Luke charged inside like a crazy midget. James Henry waddled in behind him before falling over. Lenny stepped over his child and walked directly to the fridge. Inside, his mom left him a homemade pie just like she promised she would.

"Ok guys, let's go and get you settled in," Lenny said.

It wouldn't take long. Lenny didn't pack much and he concentrated most of his suitcase on diapers.

Luke ran upstairs and Lenny walked through the kitchen to look for the car in the adjoining garage. He opened the door by the little pantry and stepped from the kitchen directly into a small garage.

He flipped the switch and there she was – his father's black and silver Ambassador convertible – locked up tightly, with less than a foot of room around all sides.

It looked as big as a tank in Mr. Long's garage but the car was only a two-seater. But Lenny loved that car. It was his father's pride and joy.

And it hardly ever left their garage.

Lenny checked to make sure the keys were in the ignition where his father always left them. It made Lenny smile to think that his father had the car always ready to go and never took it anywhere.

Lenny would take it into the city.

"Who wants to go and see some wrestling?" Lenny shouted.

There was no reply. Lenny knew the walls were thick in his parents house so he stepped back into the kitchen and asked again. Luke could hear his father but he didn't reply in the hope that Lenny mightn't ask again.

"I said, who wants to go and see some wrestling matches?"

Mickey Jack Crisp felt at odds with his surroundings. He was standing at the back of a cruising Gulf Stream II making himself a cocktail. His life was a bit like that since he started getting work from these wrestling guys. He noticed the bosses who didn't have power were running matches at high schools and bars while the one who called all the shots got champagne arrivals on private jets.

There was no in-between in the wrestling business. You were either a star or you were a nobody. You were either on top or you were simply treading water.

Not that Mickey was complaining. The stack of cash he was paid to do this job was so thick that it was uncomfortable – even split up in his various pockets. And he didn't even have to kill the guy. The old boss man said he was going to handle that – just like he did in the field with Proctor King.

Mickey was sorry to see the man who brought him into this business get his head blown off. But, like a stray dog, he was willing to go with whoever grabbed his leash and treated him well.

Cruising thousands of feet above Tennessee, sucking on a fresh strawberry would tick the 'treated well' box.

Shane sat in first class beside a very uncomfortable old lady who didn't like the look of the struggling man beside her. He was sweating profusely, moaning in pain and his bandages were struggling to keep the dirt out and the blood in.

He rolled his head towards the small rounded window and counted down the minutes 'til he landed in Dallas. Annie was all he could think about.

He would land and make this horrible situation right.

CHAPTER TWELVE

Danno sat handcuffed in the back of the police car. Both the arresting officers entered a gas station about a mile outside the airport – and failed to come back. Danno couldn't reach the door to let himself out. Ten minutes or more passed before Nestor Chapman opened Danno's door and escorted him from the patrol car.

"Say nothing and come with me," Nestor said as he uncuffed Danno and escorted him by his forearm to another, unmarked car.

Danno wasn't sure, but he wasn't fighting either.

"You're my prisoner now," Nestor informed him as he opened his passenger side door.

Danno guardedly sat in and watched Nestor do the same on his side.

"How about I drop you home?" Nestor asked.

"How about you tell me what the fuck it is you want from me?"

Nestor started his car. "Why don't we do mine first?"

Nestor backed out of the parking lot and saluted the two officers as they entered their patrol car. It was all perfectly timed, like this kind of thing happened all the time.

"You know, I'm on your side," Nestor said.

"Of course you are."

Nestor laughed a little and tapped his cigarette pack off the dashboard.

"What's so funny?" Danno asked.

Nestor offered Danno a smoke, which he refused, and then picked himself one from the pack with his lips.

"You really haven't had to think that much about my side of the fence before, have you Danno?"

"Am I under arrest or not?"

Nestor considerately rolled down his window and waved his smoke outside. "I'm like a subcontractor," Nestor proudly said. "Your guy gives me a little something to make sure you and yours stay out of trouble over my side of the fence."

Danno didn't answer. He knew well enough about talking to the cops.

"Troy. Troy Bartlett," Nestor said.

That name got Danno interested. He hadn't seen or heard from his lawyer in days. Danno was starting to think that might be a bad thing too. If the cops did have someone who was willing to roll him, Troy Bartlett wouldn't be a shock. He was a dirty lawyer with little or no morals. And that's exactly what you need when you're starting an empire. But it's the last thing you need when you're sitting atop one.

Nestor watched Danno hard to see if Troy's name knocked Danno's tongue loose.

"Hey, listen," Nestor said, starting to lose his cool a little. "I fucking put my ass on the line back there so you better stop treating me like some junkie dirtbag or something. You hear me, old man?"

Danno still wasn't talking. Nestor flicked his half-smoked cigarette out the window and reached around inside his jacket pocket.

"Here," he said as he handed Danno an envelope. "This is for you. Thought you might appreciate getting these back."

Nestor dropped the envelope in Danno's lap. "It's your wife's things. What they found on her when ... "

Danno's face contorted with anger.

"It's true, man. I'm on your side. I got a friend of mine to do me a favor and get me that. I'm trying to fucking show you."

Nestor slammed on the brakes and leaned across Danno to open his door. "Out," he said. "When you open that and see I'm not bullshitting you, you give me a call. And make it soon."

Danno got out and waited on the side of the highway as Nestor skidded off without him. Danno couldn't decide if Nestor was who he said he was. He pocketed the envelope and began walking.

Ricky sat with 'The Book' on his lap. It was full of match ideas, possible outcomes and future match-ups. The page in front of him was now full of brackets and tournament outcomes.

He was being watched closely by Tanner Blackwell and not so closely by Joe Lapine.

"What are we up to?" Tanner asked.

"The semi-finals," Ricky answered while looking at his watch.

It had been a painful few hours with negotiation after negotiation. Everyone wanted their guys to look good but someone had to lose.

"I want my guy up against a sneaky Jap," Tanner said.

Joe and Ricky looked at each other to clarify if they both heard the same thing.

"A Jap?" Joe asked. "There's no Japanese wrestlers here."

"Then fucking find one. I want to position my guy as a real

patriot. A fucking American hero," Tanner answered.

He was working on his own plan in his own 'Book'. And Tanner's 'Book' was still trading off old prejudices from the 40's.

He continued, "We have an African, a Chink, a Samoan, a German, three Americans and a Limey. So we need to lose the Samoan and make him a Jap. Same fucking eyes."

Ricky was done arguing. He just shrugged his shoulder in Joe's direction.

"Can you do that Ricky?" Joe asked.

"He's going to have to get a loan of some karate ...eh... trousers or something," Tanner said without looking up from his doodling. "And I don't like the finish of the main event either."

Ricky wasn't having that. "You don't like what, Tanner?"

"My guy should go over," Tanner replied. "On his own."

"That wasn't the deal," Ricky said. "Joe?"

Joe stood up, "We voted, Tanner. They both get the pin and a title each. That's what we decided."

Tanner rubbed out his last scenario and blew the eraser residue from his page.

Lenny Long knew his way around Madison Square Garden. He knew the people who worked there. He knew all there was to know.

But taking a baby in there might be pushing it a bit.

"Helen, please," he said through the will call window. "I just want to watch a couple of matches and then I'll come straight back."

The woman in the ticket booth was shaking her head adamantly.

Luke was grabbing his father's hand tightly. He didn't want to go anywhere without his father. James Henry was asleep in Lenny's arms despite the noise.

"I've just gotten off a flight and I haven't seen The Boys in days. I just want to … "

Lenny could see that she wasn't going to budge. He'd just have to watch his own children.

Lenny dragged his older son by the arm and guarded the baby as he passed through the rowdy fans. Under his coat he was bare-chested because he had taken off his shirt and tied it around his baby's head to stifle the noise.

"What do you think of this, son?" Lenny stooped and asked Luke.

He didn't wait for a reply as he marched them to section 422, row B, seat 4.

Lenny only got one. They'd just have to share.

The closer they got to their seat the more the crowd thinned out. Hugely. Lenny was taken aback by how small the crowd was in the mezzanine level. The ringside was tight and looked good, but the further up the seating they went the worse it got.

"How long are we going to be here?" Luke asked with his hands on his ears.

Even with the small crowd, chants and cheers rattled around in The Garden like noisy, aggressive, old ghosts.

They had just made it in time for the main event. Lenny opened his program, like someone starving might look at a menu. It had only been days since he was around this world, but to Lenny it was days too long. He immediately saw the confusing graphic of Babu listed as heavyweight champion. The last time Lenny saw Babu, just five days before, he was to drop the belt to Proctor King in Florida.

Lenny had no idea about how much had truly changed since he left Florida that night to start his new life away from wrestling.

The curtain flung open and out came the giant frame of the man Lenny now knew as Chrissy. To this audience he was the most despised man in all of wrestling – undefeated for years and likely to be so for more years to come. But more recently, and much more importantly to the New York crowd, he was the one who recently no-showed the biggest main event of all time. Years of buildup and bad feeling. A stadium packed to the rafters.

And he simply didn't show up.

What they didn't know was his no-show had zero to do with him. And the rules of wrestling meant they would never know.

The Garden's small house was a 'fuck you' to the champion and the company he wrestled for. And as if the point hadn't been made enough they also threw cups of liquid and trash at him as he ambled up the wooden steps and through the ropes.

"Go fuck yourself you cowardly bastard," roared someone from behind Lenny.

"Champ?" Lenny shouted, even though he knew there was no way Babu could hear him. "Champ?"

"Ring the bell before he chickens out of the match ref," shouted another.

It was always good for the heel to rile the crowd. That's what they were there for. That was their job. And they would do almost anything to get that heat from the stands.

But Babu was the owner of 'bad heat'.

That was the kind of reaction that no wrestler wanted. People would pay for 'good heat.' The kind where you would pay to see someone get their ass kicked. That's 'good heat'.

'Bad heat' was the other kind. The kind where a crowd just doesn't want to see you or walks to the concession stand when you come through the curtain. Or worse – stays home. 'Bad heat' gets a low card wrestler fired, a mid-card wrestler sent to another territory and a champion wrestler stripped of the belt.

"Ladies and gentlemen," said the ring announcer into the hanging mic. "This is the feature attraction of the evening, and is one fall to a finish. Introducing to you now, first, the challenger. From Orange County, Florida. Weighing in at two hundred and eighty four pounds. Flawless Fargo."

The crowd clapped respectfully. Fargo was up from Florida and no one in The Garden knew who he was.

The ring announcer with the pot belly and slicked-back hair continued. "And in the other corner, The World Heavyweight Champion. Coming to you from deepest, darkest South Africa. And weighing in at four hundred and fifty pounds. BABUUUUUUU."

The crowd lost it. They paid their ticket just to see Babu and tell him how much they fucking hated him.

The bell at ringside sounded over and over to try and start the match. But Lenny knew that Chrissy, the man everyone else knew as Babu, wasn't happy.

Lenny's own shouting towards the ring had his baby boy in floods of tears. His tiny mind couldn't seem to process why it was so dark and so angry.

Lenny never even noticed.

"Dad?" Luke said.

Lenny continued to chant and whoop as the bell rang.

"Dad?" Luke repeated and pulled on his father's sleeve.

Lenny looked down to see his eldest son's face.

"Look," Luke said, pointing at his little brother.

Lenny saw James Henry in distress. He was tired and his face was red and warm. Lenny desperately wanted to stay. He wanted to find out what was happening and why The Garden was so empty. He wanted to see Danno and Ricky.

He wanted back in.

Lenny walked from The Garden with his little boys both quietly sucking on stacked popsicles. He was feeling slightly hard done by, but not enough to be angry or anything. Fact was, after years on the road and having no responsibilities as a father, things changed.

He wasn't any good at it yet, but he wanted to be. He wanted to be a wise father, someone they both sought out when life began to settle into its normal patterns for them. He even felt a little good about leaving the match. He felt like a grown-up. A grown-up trying to do the right thing by his family.

As he carried one son and let the other swing from his arm, Lenny felt like his father must have felt before him. He felt like a man. A proper, solid, doing-what-he-should man.

And for once in his life toughness had nothing to do with it.

CHAPTER THIRTEEN

Five days after the murder.

Texas.

Shane couldn't break through the hedging at the back of Curt's house. It was just too thick, and there wasn't a single gap down low, so he found himself trying to scale it – quietly.

The agony in his foot had brought a feverish sweat out on his face. He was tired and tortured and determined to surprise the man who signed him, wooed him, ignored him, conned him and threatened him.

He needed to get in there before Danno arrived.

And he knew that couldn't be far from happening.

He clasped two hopeful fists of green and hoisted himself atop the large hedging which began to wobble and make far too much noise. He had no choice but to throw his leg over and fall into the garden. The paved portion of the garden.

Shane lay numb with pain and tried desperately to refill his totally emptied lungs.

As he lay there he wasn't at all sure exactly which part of him was the sorest.

One day before the murder.

Texas.

Curt Magee and Shane Montrose sat opposite each other in a small steakhouse about a hundred miles outside of Austin. It was small and smoky and the sauces sat hardened at the top of their glass bottles.

Shane sat with his head dropped. Not in all his years as a wrestling star had the Sugarstick hoped to be *not* noticed. But it's amazing how a huge loan and a serious money lender can turn an extrovert inwards.

"I have to wear a fucking leisure suit, Curt," Shane mumbled under his breath. "Do you know what it's like for me to have to wear this shit? I feel like a fucking failed cheerleader or something. Some fucking track goon or something."

The waitress slipped a dry steak supper under both of their noses and then smiled at Shane before she left.

"Where's my money?" Shane demanded to know.

"Tomorrow."

"Tomorrow?"

"Yeah."

"What time?"

"Eight. I'll pick you up," Curt said.

Curt could tell by Shane's twitchiness that he was not happy.

"How do you think I feel? Huh? I'm fucking losing everything here," Curt said. "I have Danno, the fat prick, buying me out of business just so I can pay your fucking contract."

"He's buying *us* out of business," Shane replied.

Curt shook his head, mumbled to himself and cut into his steak.

"What are you saying?" Shane asked.

"I'm saying that it seems to be *our* business when we're about to sell. It was *my* business when all the bills had to be paid."

"It's *our* business. We had a deal." Shane slid the plate away in disgust and lit up another cigarette.

"We wouldn't have to sell at all if you weren't fucking his wife," Curt mumbled.

Shane heard that one. "You're selling up because you're a terrible promoter. You had a gift in me down here. I was a fucking star and you're dithering... "

"Dithering?"

"Yeah, fucking dithering."

"Is that even a word?"

"Yes it's a word. What do you mean is it a word? Did you hear it come out of my ass? No? It's a fucking word then. 'Cause it came out of my mouth."

"Okay."

"Dither is a word."

"Okay, I said."

Shane reset his thoughts and tried again. "You've been too soft for the last two years. Waiting on Danno's good graces. You should have pulled on him harder."

Curt banged his fork handle off the table. "I could have had a golden ring with money falling out of the ceiling down here and Danno wasn't going to do business with me. It had nothing to do with my skills. I asked you. I asked you when we were putting this deal together if there was anything I should know."

"Yeah? And?"

"And? And? You were fucking the man's wife."

Shane felt a little trapped by that reality. "How was I supposed to know he knew? Did you want me to ask him? Did you want me to check with him to see if he knew that I was boning his sweetheart before I signed with you?"

Curt slid his plate away. "I can't wait to get out of this fucking business. I've lost my house, my company, my wife, my kids. And then I have you putting a gun to my fucking head to pay you on a contract that we shook on years ago. I couldn't make the match. You know that. You saw what Danno was like. Fucking intent on making sure that match *didn't* happen. Why are you ... "

Shane leaned in good and close. He had a battered and terrified wife waiting for him and a kid in shock, refusing to speak. He had some very serious men looking to track him down. He just wasn't in the mood to chit-chat or patter backwards and forwards about who's further up shit creek.

"I gave you time," Shane said very deliberately. "I took money from people to feed my family on your good word ... "

"You took money to fuck, gamble and fly around like Mr. Millionaire. My family home was sold so you could shove it up your nose," Curt said.

Shane continued at a deliberate pace. "On your word. On your word I got that money loaned to me. It doesn't fucking matter what I did with it." He slid back his chair and stood up. "Make this right tomorrow. I haven't got anymore time left to dodge these people. Because I promise that if you try to fuck me over with the payoff, I will make sure that whatever happens to my family happens ten times back to yours."

Shane pulled his collar up.

"That's right, leave me to handle one last bill, you prick," Curt said as he watched Shane leave.

The day of the murder.

Texas.

He had been everywhere and dined with everyone. He had ridden in the best transportation the world had to offer. He wore the finest clothes money could buy. He became successful in his life without being able to read or write to a large degree. There was nothing decadent on earth that he hadn't fucked, ate, smoked, snorted or bought.

But this day, Shane Montrose woke in the back of a broken-down secondhand hatchback on the side of an unknown Texas road.

He opened the door and fell out onto the dusty ground. The sun focused down right on the top of his head which made him sick and dizzy. He stood with his dick in his hand and willed it to work. Just a little. Just a trickle. Anything. Where one part of his body refused to discard fluid, another, his mouth, was way more helpful. He had nothing of substance in his stomach so a swirl of acidic water projected from his lips and darkened the dust around his feet.

He didn't even bother to try and avoid it. He just stood there with his dick in his hand puking stomach water all over himself.

His shoes, his suit ruined. His pockets empty. His family were terrified and he felt he was just a couple of hours away from ending up on the other side of that dust under his feet.

His stomach quickly and violently heaved and pulled him the opposite direction. He struggled to open his belt in time and squat. No paper either.

"Fuck," he said with absolutely no conviction.

He was too beat. Too tired. Too hung over. Too jittery.

Curt walked into the hotel bar. He knew today was the day that he makes the deal to get the fuck out of the wrestling business. The time was right. On top of the shit that naturally comes with being a boss, Curt also knew that Danno had been paying his local TV station double what Curt had just to keep Curt's wrestling show *off* the air.

Danno was essentially, and effectively, killing Curt's Texas territory from New York – and without starting another war.

Without TV Curt couldn't reach the homes to promote his stars to get people excited enough to buy tickets.

No TV equals no business.

But Curt knew Danno wasn't having it all his own way either. He listened with delight when Tanner Blackwell told him over the phone how Danno had just fucked up the biggest match of all time in Shea Stadium.

Such misery should have brought a great smile to Curt's face. But he thought that if Danno had just listened to him and his proposal for a main event everything would have been alright. They both would have been rich. Instead, now they were scheduled to meet in Texas so Danno could pay him bottom dollar for his wrestling company that hadn't functioned properly in years.

Either way, Curt was just happy to be able to get enough money to pay his debts and break out of it with a couple of grand for himself.

All he had to do was get the money before Shane Montrose found him.

Shane was past the point of giving a fuck about anything. He had traveled just a couple of miles down the road and was standing in a musty phone box just outside a tiny town he didn't recognize.

His vomit was drying into his clothes, he was sucking on a raw bottle of vodka and had a white ring around his left nostril.

"Hello?" Shane said belligerently to the answering voice.

"Who's this?" Grobie asked from the other end of the line.

Shane was expecting Curt. "Sorry, Mrs. Magee. It's Shane Montrose. I was looking for your son."

"What's this *Mrs. Magee* shit? You know me more intimately than that?"

As if Shane wasn't feeling sick enough.

"Have you seen him … Grobie?"

"He should be there by now," she replied, slightly confused. "He left here about fifteen minutes ago."

Shane knew she was getting her wires crossed somewhere and instinctively went with it. "He left already?"

"Yeah, unless he stopped somewhere for gas or something," she replied.

"Okay," Shane said unable to think of a way to reply properly.

He was about to hang up and try to digest what he'd just heard when Grobie chimed back in again.

"Are you two coming back here to celebrate after? I can roast you a chicken or something?"

Shane was trying to figure out what was going on.

"You could come by yourself anytime. You know that, right?" she asked.

"What? Yeah. Of course."

Shane's broken brain pieced together the scant information. A meeting happening now, fifteen minutes from Grobie's house. He needed more.

"Maybe we could bring back a bottle from here?" he asked, totally unsure of her potential answer.

"That would be perfect," she said.

Shane hung up and ran back to his shitty car. Whatever was going down, it was happening right now and he wasn't even sure how far from the meeting point he was.

Annie made her way down to the hotel bar, carrying the rucksack full of money. This was what she wanted, a piece of business to handle to help her husband get through this.

The bar was quiet and mostly empty. She looked out for a man her husband had described as "a really brown fucker with a white mustache and shaky hands."

Annie scrutinized the room and ordered a drink. Curt sat by the window and kept a nervous eye out for Shane Montrose. The last thing he needed was him showing up and embarrassing, or derailing, the deal.

"Curt?" asked a lady's voice.

"Yes?" Curt answered, a little confused.

Annie Garland offered a handshake and Curt obliged while standing up.

"Hello. I'm Annie Garland. I think we met briefly in New York at a party," she said as she sat down at the table.

Curt thought that maybe Annie was in town with Danno and was just saying hello on her way through. "Oh yes, Mrs. Garland. Your anniversary party. I'm sorry; I wasn't expecting to see you down here. I was in a world of my own. Has your husband been delayed?"

"He's not coming," Annie answered.

"Excuse me?"

"As you may know, my husband is otherwise engaged tonight. Although he is anxious to complete the deal before the main event begins later."

Curt couldn't believe that Danno would disrespect him again. He stood up. "I'm sorry, darling, but this is a slap in the face to me and a waste of my fucking time."

"Sit down, Mr. Magee, or the deal will be pulled immediately," Annie said, while opening the rucksack. She noticed an envelope on top that said '**Sorry**' in someone's handwriting.

"Excuse me?" Curt said.

"I said there will be no second go-around here today or any other, Mr. Magee. My husband's offer expires the second you leave this bar."

Curt struggled to contain his contempt for the power this woman seemed to have over him. "What's going on here? I thought we had a deal? I have a line of people who are looking for payments from me, Mrs. Garland. Going out of business is not a cheap pursuit."

Curt couldn't resist looking out the window for the number one person in the line.

"We want to do a deal," Annie said.

He knew he hadn't got the time to grandstand. What else could he do only sit back into the seat like a lobster being eased into a pot.

"And he gave you full permission to make the decisions to get this deal done?" Curt asked.

Annie was intrigued by the envelope and opened it under the table. Inside there were two ladies rings. One looked to be an engagement ring and the other a wedding ring.

"I don't want to prolong this humiliation any further, Mrs. Garland. Your husband promised me a cash deal here today." Curt's nerves were beginning to show on his face. It looked to Annie like both of his hands were shaking now.

Annie quickly pocketed the rings and read the note that accompanied them:

I'm sorry boss. I don't have all the money. I will pay you back. I promise. I'm sorry. Lenny.

"Is there a problem?" Curt asked, starting to get nervous and a little paranoid as to what Annie was silently reading under the table.

Annie knew now she didn't have the money to make the deal. At a bar in Texas, both Annie and Curt were starting to feel the pressure of this deal.

Shane crisscrossed all the bars and restaurants within fifteen minutes from Grobie's house. He knew the ones Curt liked to drink in, but there was no sign of him. He waited for the red lights to turn green. Another opportunity to burn through some coke.

He tried to focus on what he knew. Curt wasn't going to bring Danno to a shitty bar. He was going to try and impress him. Make Danno think that he was a big-shot owner.

He knew, there and then, where Curt was.

Annie counted the remaining blocks of cash in a stall in the ladies room. Eighty four thousand. Saying she had eighty four thousand made her look like an amateur. A round, concise number conveyed the confidence that she was acting from. She composed herself and packed seventy back into the rucksack. The rest, she crammed into her purse.

Out in the bar, Curt was still waiting at the table. That alone led Annie to believe that this deal wasn't dead. He looked sweaty and twitchy and constantly scanned the room.

"My apologies, Curt. Had to … "

Curt was far past Annie's faux charm. "I want a hundred and twenty thousand now, Mrs. Garland. Your husband's disrespect toward me has been shocking and upsetting, quite frankly. He and I have served together on the National Wrestling Council for … "

"I'm going to give you seventy thousand now, Curt. You get less for being an asshole."

The original deal was for ninety thousand. Curt tried his luck in demanding an extra thirty grand. Annie tried to assert her dominance by cutting him by twenty.

Curt laughed. "This is why I don't deal with the wives, Mrs. Garland. They are crazy one hundred percent of the time."

"If you disrespect me one more time, I will pull the money from this deal altogether."

Shane pulled his dying car into a spot at the edge of the parking lot. He surveyed the area and spotted Curt's car parked around the side of the hotel, away from prying eyes.

He was positive he was being cut out of a deal again. A deal that could save his life; that could save his family's lives.

He was too old not to collect on every penny that his broken down body could make him and deals like the one he signed with Curt Magee would never come around for him again.

Shane Montrose wanted what was his.

He left his car and stooped and staggered underneath the windows of the hotel bar. He wanted to scout the 'get together' and see what was happening.

He cowered behind a parked truck and took stock of the patrons in the hotel bar through the window. Inside he could see Curt's back, but couldn't see much past him. Shane's position was all wrong.

He moved again to try and get a better angle but he was drawn to the slap of the bar door closing. He saw Curt leaving in a hurry. Shane ducked down and watched him marching towards his car but Curt veered over to the parking lot payphone instead. Shane was about to get up and challenge Curt but the sight of Annie Garland beyond the glass hotel door stopped him dead in his tracks.

Annie?

Shane stooped back down again, almost unable to take in what he was seeing. He never in a million years thought that Annie would be in a deal that would fuck him over. But nothing surprised him in the wrestling business.

She walked outside and went quickly up the steps to her room on the second floor. To Shane it looked like she was trying to avoid being seen. To Annie she just wanted to get back to her room quickly and safely. The end of her meeting didn't go well. Curt knocked the glasses off the table and left in a rage. She wasn't going to take any chances.

At the payphone Curt watched Annie take to her room.

"Hello, you have reached the New York Booking Agency, the home of the word's greatest wrestling attractions. We are unable to come to the phone right now so please leave a message. Thank you."

Beep.

Curt slammed the phone off the glass before dialing again. Another answering machine. This time with no message. It was Danno's house machine.

Beep.

Curt didn't even know where to start. "Danno," he blurted out. "You fucking fat piece of shit. Sending your fucking wife down was an insult. You know that, Danno? She's a fucking whore. Who do you think you are trying to stiff me at the last minute? You bring down the money we agreed. That was the deal. Not some light fucking number you made up. The deal. You made a deal."

Danno's offer, Danno's wife and Danno squeezing him out of the business made Curt feel small-time. On his own. Isolated is a bad place to be in the wrestling business.

"And if you think I'm going to take this lying down ... well, fuck you."

Curt slammed the phone down.

Shane watched Curt, from the other end of the parking lot, get into his car and drive off at speed. Shane had no idea what to think. He couldn't figure out what the angle was.

Who was fucking who?

Seeing Annie Garland walk from the lobby and take the outside stairs to her room made him think it was him who was taking it in the ass. From the fucking promoters and their backstabbing and throat slitting. And from the woman who told him she loved him.

"She was in on it all along," he could only mumble to himself. "That fucking bitch was in it all along."

Half a mile down the road and Curt Magee could hardly control his anger. He was shaking with adrenaline and his mind was wild with scenes of Danno, and maybe even the other bosses, laughing at him. He couldn't go home empty-handed. He *wouldn't* go home empty handed.

Curt slammed on the brakes and turned his car around.

He was going to teach Danno a lesson.

Five days after the murder.

Texas.

Curt was restless. For days he was waking up constantly with the feeling that he could go back to the way it was. Make all this better. He could do things differently. He hated being on the run. He just wanted out of this fucking business for good.

He rolled from his right hip onto his left hip and punched his pillow into comfort. But an immediate chill ran along his spine as he sensed someone else in the room with him. His eyes shot open and he could see a hooded Shane Montrose kneeling at the head of his bed.

"What the fuck are you ... " Curt tried to ask before Shane

grabbed Curt's mouth and drove a kitchen knife into his neck repeatedly.

But Curt still gargled and struggled.

Shane, now panicked and shocked, began to just hack at Curt's neck as the blood flowed and gushed from several different areas, spraying up into Shane's face. He leaned over and pressed his elbow into Curt's face as he stabbed his stomach area and furiously punched him in the face.

Curt stopped suddenly and it was deathly quiet.

Except for footsteps behind him.

Shane jumped up and pushed past a paralyzed Grobie standing in shock behind him. Shane sprinted as fast as his foot would allow him. He tried to take the stairs too many at a time and fell to the bottom. He felt his forearm snap when he hit the last step.

He could hear movement upstairs as he scrambled to his feet. He dragged himself along the hallway and into the kitchen. He swung open the back door and knew straight away that he couldn't climb that fence again. Especially with a broken arm. He changed direction and limped along the side of the house and out onto the street.

CHAPTER FOURTEEN

The day of the murder.

Texas.

Curt pulled into a free spot and launched himself from his seat. His legs carried him up the steps two at a time. He didn't know what he was going to do but he was going to make sure that no one took him for a fucking pushover again. If today was his last day in the wrestling business, he was going to make sure that each and every one of those bastards who were left would remember him for a long time to come.

Curt walked up to Annie's door and pounded on it. He knew there was no way she was going to answer it. So he tried to bust his way in.

"Annie," he shouted with his forehead on the door. "You let me in."

The room was quiet. Curt checked to make sure he had the right door. It was definitely the one he saw her enter earlier. Maybe she checked out already. Maybe she made a run for it.

Curt scrutinized the parking lot for movement or anything suspicious.

All this game playing was just making him worse. He had one last quick look around and threw a kick at the door.

His heart was pumping and, such was his anger, he was having a hard time unballing his fists.

"Annie?" he said as he kicked again. The door shot open with the force of his foot and Curt saw Annie lying on the floor, already clearly dead.

He backed out slowly and ran for his life. His shouting and kicking the door drew many people to see him flee.

Five minutes before the murder.

Texas.

Annie Garland collected the few things she had together and threw them into her bag. She didn't know what she was going to tell her husband. She made a huge mess of the one deal he ever trusted her with.

As cool as she played it with Curt, she feared for her safety in Texas. Annie wasn't used to the type of anger that Curt showed at the end of the meeting. She was sure her husband could pull something together in the end, but she wanted to close the deal herself.

She took out two pills and lay them in her cupped hand, before downing them with a drink of water. She felt the rings and note in her pocket. Annie thought she would bring the rings back home and quietly return them to Lenny. Danno didn't have to know.

"Annie?" whispered a familiar voice from outside the door.

Even his voice made her feel a certain way. A way she had a hard time explaining. But it was a way she was instantly attracted to. She pressed her eye to the door and saw a distorted version of Shane Montrose looking left and right outside. She cracked open the door and let him in.

He clearly needed a shower and looked disheveled. His clothes were stained and his eyes were red raw. Annie had never really seen him like this before.

"What are you doing here?" she asked.

"What are *you* doing here?" he asked in return. His version of the question was loaded and paranoid.

Annie took seriously the instructions to not let anyone know about the deal. It wasn't to be announced to anyone in case one of the other bosses were to swoop in and pick over the bones for a quarter of the price.

"I was just… visiting a friend. A girlfriend from college," she lied.

Shane approached too fast and too threatening for her liking.

"I fucking saw you out there with him," Shane said. His teeth were clenched and his eyes were saucer wide. Annie saw a fraction of this before. She saw him go wild. He would punch some table and flex his muscles. Get into a brawl. Ten minutes later he would hold her gentle to his chest and try to explain why he did what he did. He always failed to put into words why he did what he did, but a man like Shane Montrose got real good at learning how to apologize the right way.

He grabbed her wrists. "Answer me, Annie. What are you doing down here?"

"It's none of your business what I do," she said as she struggled free. "What right have you got to ask me anything like that?"

"You're in on this with them, aren't you?"

"What?"

"Your fat fuck of a husband is pulling you back in, is he?"

Annie walked to the door but Shane stood in her path.

"I want you to leave. Now," she said, her voice dropping with fright.

Annie turned her back on him and he grabbed her hair and yanked her onto the bed.

"Were you in on this from the start? Were you part of them cutting me out of this?"

Shane followed her eyes as she instinctively looked towards the bag full of money. He could make out the faintest sight of the bills on top.

They both dived for the bag and grabbed a handle each. Annie refused to let go.

"That's my fucking money," he shouted and lashed out, slapping her across the face.

They both paused in shock. Her face began to sting from the impact of his hand. She had never been hit before.

"I'm sorry," he pleaded.

Annie rose to her feet and walked quickly for the door. He couldn't let her go. He needed to make it right before she got back to Danno. Money and backstabbing was all fair play. But hitting the boss's wife? That would get you killed.

"Annie?" He walked into her path again. Her right cheek was red-raw and there were tears coming from her eyes.

"They are going to kill my family, Annie. Please."

"Move," she said trying not to cry in front of him.

"My little girl. I have to get the money. They've been to my house."

Annie wasn't listening. Or didn't care anymore. Either way, Shane knew if she crossed that door he was dead.

He stepped aside and she fumbled nervously with the lock. She was sure it turned right to open. He pulled her back forcefully and cranked his arm under her chin and clasped his hands shut at the side of her head.

She struggled a little in silence. She couldn't move much or make any noise. His grip left her helpless. She could only kick her legs and try in vain to unlock his hands. His grip was simply debilitating after a few seconds.

They both lay on her bed. In silence. They both knew she was dying. They both waited for it to happen. They both cried.

Her body was unresponsive but her mind knew exactly what was happening.

She violently jerked and tried one last time to free herself. Then she went limp. He let her go and guided her sliding body softly onto the floor.

Shane took a second. He wiped his eyes and looked at her.

He shook the money from her purse and stacked it on top of the money in the rucksack.

He then left.

CHAPTER FIFTEEN

Five days after the murder.

Texas.

Mickey Jack turned down the top of Curt's street and immediately saw the ambulances and police cars scattered around. All their lights were flashing in the dark and there were people starting to gather to see what was happening.

"Just continue, I have the wrong place," Mickey Jack said to his cab driver.

He checked the address he got from Danno with the house that was surrounded and knew it was the one.

He seemed to have a knack for turning up with the job already done.

He snuck a look through the back window and could see a covered body being wheeled out of the house. A local news truck was also unloading its equipment as the cab turned the corner.

"Where to now?" the cab driver asked.

"Take me back to the airport," Mickey said, sliding a five dollar bill between the front seats.

Six days after the murder.

New York.

Joe Lapine never fucking liked the phone ringing when he was asleep. That stupid fucking phone, fucking ringing and giving him a fucking heart attack.

"What?" he shouted down the line.

"Are you on your own?" Tanner Blackwell asked in a very matter-of-fact way.

Joe threw the phone against the wall and begrudgingly put on his glasses. He knew ten seconds in that this day was going to be a terrible day. He rose and fumbled around for the light switch. It was late afternoon but his room had ceiling-to-floor heavy curtains blocking the daylight out.

It had been a long night for Joe. A long, great fucking night.

"Move it," he grunted to the woman in his bed. She didn't move nearly fast enough out of the room.

"Chop, chop, sweetheart," he said as he stomped around the bed and clapped his hands like he was trying to scare chickens out of his way.

With the room now empty and the curtains pulled back, Joe sat on the edge of his bed.

"You there, Joe?" Tanner shouted down the line.

Joe picked up the phone and put it to his ear. "Yeah?"

"I just got a phone call from Texas. We have to settle this now," Tanner said.

Across town, Ricky was nodding off in his chair while Ginny took a shower. Ricky kinda liked not having to talk sometimes so he'd put on something loud and distracting. He liked his day after a

Garden card to be without fuss – an all too infrequent thing these days.

Joe sat distressed in his hotel room chair.

"So, one of the wrestlers Curt fucked over on a payoff called one of my guys, who called me," Tanner said, explaining how he knew what he knew.

"Are you sure it's Curt?"

Tanner was getting annoyed at how little of a fuck his chairman seemed to give. "Yes, it's all over the TV down there. His goddamn mother gave an eyewitness account that it was Shane-fucking-Montrose they were looking for."

Tanner paused and his voice went cold for a couple of seconds. "Just tell me that you're sorting this now. We warned Garland to stay away from Texas."

"And how do you know Danno was behind this?"

"Don't give me that shit Joe. You know what has to happen here. I need to be protected. I'm fucking in with Danno and the title situation up to my ass."

Joe was genuinely hurt by what he was about to do. "I got it," he said.

"You've got an hour," Tanner warned him. "You handle it within an hour or I do."

Joe grew tired of Tanner's questions and demands. "I fucking got it," he said as he slammed the phone down.

In that instant, Joe Lapine from Memphis, Tennessee found himself tasked with the job of protecting the wrestling business and making sure it sustained no more damage. He was left with zero option. Danno was *making* him deal with him. He was *making* him do something. For nearly a hundred years the wrestling business kept its mouth shut, put its head down and just made money. Joe knew that they couldn't let one man – Danno Garland – ruin all that.

So he quickly got dressed and made his way across the huge hotel suite where last night's date was waiting patiently on a seat.

"So what do I tell my husband?" the young woman asked as Joe scuttled her out the door.

"Tell him to call my office in a couple of days."

"So you're going to hire him? He could be a champion, I'm telling you."

Joe pulled the door closed and walked past the woman like they never met. He entered the elevator and managed to make eye contact with four other patrons without smiling or making small talk. Ding. Out onto the marble floor and across the nearly empty lobby, through the large revolving door and out into the New York hustle to the payphone on the corner.

He took a small contacts book from his back pocket and fingered through the pages as the city pushed and pulled its inhabitants up and down stream.

He dialed in a number and waited a few rings until the voice kicked in, "Hello, you have reached the New York Booking Agency, the home … "

Joe hung up and quickly went to his book again. He dialed. The Chairman needed to deal with the issue or he in turn would be dealt with.

"Hello?" answered the voice on the other end of the line.

"Hello," Joe replied.

"Joe?" Ricky asked. "What do you want?"

Joe heard Ricky's TV blaring in the background

"You got a big fucking problem here. You want to turn that down?" Joe asked.

"What problem?"

Joe didn't even know where to start. But he knew he didn't have time to sugarcoat anything. "Curt was killed. It was down in Texas and they've got Shane Montrose."

Ricky's day off was ruined. "It was Shane?"

"I was hoping you could tell me," Joe snapped back.

"What?"

"What's he gone and done, Ricky?" Joe asked with regret.

"I don't know. I don't know what he's doing out there anymore," Ricky said honestly. He was tired of defending Danno. He knew the whole business heard Danno put a bounty on Curt Magee.

What was left that Ricky could do?

"I can tell you what's coming next," Joe said. "Tanner is going to set the cops on him."

Joe felt like he was betraying another boss by talking to Ricky and giving him a heads-up. But he liked Danno and appreciated Danno giving him the Chairman position.

"Why?" Ricky asked. "What does that do?"

"He knows Danno is where all the poison is coming from. He wants to serve him up, make him the reason for all this stuff, and make all this go away in one fell swoop."

Ricky tried to interrupt but Joe stopped him.

"He's finished. I'm sorry," Joe said.

Ricky needed more time to think. He had never come across a situation where someone from within the NWC was talking about ratting another boss to the cops. Ricky wondered whether Mickey Jack Crisp was trustworthy. He wondered if Mickey did what he paid him to do.

"What's he going to say, Joe? I need to know what's coming," Ricky said.

"Don't you waste time trying to fix this, Ricky. Tell Danno to run and get the fuck out yourself if you can."

"What's he going to say?"

"Ricky? I swear to God … "

Ricky threw down the phone and bolted from his apartment.

Joe put his phone down and watched as New York struggled past outside. It was dirty, grimy and packed with panhandlers, whores and junkies. He wanted to go home to Tennessee where he could breathe clean air.

New York was nothing but a fucking headache.

He waited by the phone in a full suit and his shoes still tied. Danno had been sitting there all night and all day wondering when Mickey Jack Crisp was going to call from Texas. He used the empty time to imagine what it would be like to pump a bullet into the man who killed his wife. With no one around, and his thoughts all to himself, Danno knew that having to kill again sickened him and frightened him.

But what else could he do? How else could he begin to make it right? Not doing anything was having a much worse effect on him than doing something. And that's where he found himself. With no real good option. Danno only had the terrible choice of killing again or the unbearable option of not.

The shrill sound of his phone finally ringing jumped him out of his thoughts in the sharpest way.

"Hello?" he said in a hurried voice.

"It's me," Mickey answered.

"Where the fuck were you?" Danno snapped.

"It's not a good situation down here."

"Have you got him?"

Mickey paused as he tried to figure out what to say next.

"What is it?" Danno asked.

"Do you want to make your way to another phone and call me back or something?" Mickey asked.

Danno didn't care. "No."

Mickey drew a couple of pained breaths and stuttered his way into a poorly constructed line. "I don't know … "

Danno could wait no longer. "Fucking say it."

"He's dead."

"What did you do?" Danno shouted angrily.

"Not me. They're saying on the news that they're holding Shane Montrose in connection with it."

"What?" Danno asked in disbelief.

"I'm watching the local news. Shane Montrose. They've got a picture of him up on the screen now. They arrested him a couple of miles from the house."

Danno couldn't process what he was hearing. How did Shane get down there? How did he know where he was?

"I got to go," Mickey said.

"Wait."

"What?"

"He's dead?" Danno asked disbelievingly.

Mickey hung up.

Danno sat with the phone to his ear and tried to digest what had happened. What was he supposed to do now? How was he going to make right his wife's memory?

Danno heard a car approaching and he lifted himself from the couch and checked the window. A black and silver Ambassador drove towards his house.

Danno hurried and took up residence behind his front door. He heard the footsteps approaching.

"Hello? You there? Boss?" Lenny shouted as he knocked on the front door.

Lenny?

Danno took a breath before opening the door slowly. Lenny was standing there smiling with his arms out.

"I ... knew you were here," Lenny blurted out.

Danno couldn't help but smile back. He felt overjoyed at seeing the harmless Lenny Long standing in front of him.

"I just wanted to say hello," Lenny said as he walked cautiously towards his former boss. "And I wanted to set something right."

Lenny had the missing money in the back of his car.

Danno dropped his head a little when he felt his lip quiver. He put out his arms and Lenny, totally confused as to what was happening, moved quicker into Danno's embrace.

"I'm so happy to see you," Danno said sincerely. "I'm so happy you're okay."

Danno compressed Lenny's slight frame and lifted him off the ground. Lenny could see that Danno was far more happy to see him now than he ever was when he worked for him.

"I thought you were dead," Danno said holding Lenny at arms length. "I thought ... "

Danno became emotional. But he stopped himself from crying.

"I'm not dead, boss. I should have said something to you. I was going to call when we got settled. Me and the family."

Danno didn't care. He just wanted another hug.

Mickey Jack Crisp stood in Dallas Airport with more money than he knew what to do with. He could maybe go home to Florida and set up something. A little business, or use the money for a deposit on a house or something. He would more than likely use it for no good. Maybe get some girls. Definitely get some girls.

"Whatever you have left will be fine," Mickey Jack said at the airport rent-a-car desk.

Danno's chartered plane waited for him somewhere on the runway outside, but Mickey just wanted to get back to Florida. He didn't want to get any further in with those wrestling guys. They were all at war, and it was hard for Mickey to know which horse to back in that race.

He had cash stuffed and taped all over his body. A car would be easier. A day or two to Gainesville, then he could fade into obscurity.

Mickey Jack Crisp had earned his money and he did what he was paid to do.

Kinda.

CHAPTER SIXTEEN

Troy Bartlett was four days in various hold cages. He was moved constantly from precinct to precinct and kept in the dark as to why he was picked up – or what they were holding him for.

Although, even with all his clients, he knew it was because he was Danno Garland's lawyer.

For the first couple of days he tried threatening the cops. But he knew they didn't give a fuck about the law. Then he tried reasoning. Then he gave up. Just sat there. Wondering. Trying to piece together what was going on.

From one shitty green precinct to another. The constant sound of filing cabinets opening and closing and typewriters being pecked at. Phones ringing. Cars starting and parking outside.

All Troy was told was there was no room for him in whatever division and he would be moved again. Precinct to precinct, with nobody talking.

But he knew it was connected to Danno.

Troy had been around enough departments, heard enough stories and paid enough envelopes to know what the bent cops looked like.

And he knew he was being tailed. Particularly when it was business to do with Danno Garland. Troy hoped the tail would go when Danno's senate hearing was over. He was wrong.

Katy Spence, the red-haired lady that convinced Danno she was Troy's broke secretary, stood outside the holding room. She was dressed in full police department uniform.

Katy entered the room.

"How are you today Troy?" she asked as she sat by the side of the wire mesh cage.

Troy had enough. He owed nobody nothing in this world. Not even Danno Garland. He had been tight-lipped for days but he wasn't made for this. He was a meticulous man who couldn't abide imposition. He wasn't tough or street smart, and didn't want to be. He was paid to be a different kind of smart. A type of smart that he knew one day could end him up exactly where he was.

"I last spoke to Danno Garland less than two weeks ago. On October first," he said without much prompting.

Katy was taken a little off guard by Troy's candor. She had been trying to get him to talk for days but he always resisted. Maybe he had simply been stewing for long enough.

Troy continued. "It was the day before the senate hearings. He didn't know how it was going to go. He didn't know what was going to happen. He was stashing all his cash in bags and running around his house packing up valuables."

"And what did you talk about?" Katy asked.

She felt slightly out of her depth but she didn't want Troy to stop now that he started.

"I need to get out of here," Troy said. "I think I'm losing my fucking mind."

"I can arrange that after a few more questions," Katy replied.

In an ordinary case moving in an ordinary direction, there would be no way a rookie like Katy would be let near a witness.

But there was nothing ordinary about this at all.

"The last piece of business I had with Danno was a pre-emptive and hasty meeting in the barn beside his house. He wanted to move his businesses out of his own name just in case the government decided to go after him."

Twelve days before.

New York.

Danno threw his father's picture on the bed. He clicked open the safe and dragged the blocks of cash onto a waiting bedsheet on the floor.

In the kitchen, he pulled out the drawers and dipped his arm into the body of the cabinets and pulled out more bags of cash.

In the barn, he hurriedly pulled more money that was wrapped in plastic from the bales of hay.

"Annie?" he shouted as he rushed through the barn doors.

"Danno?" said a male voice from behind. Danno stopped dead and waited for something.

"Danno?" the voice repeated.

It sounded familiar so Danno felt better about turning. Behind him stood his no-nonsense, grey-faced lawyer, Troy Bartlett. "I've got the papers you asked for. Is everything okay?"

Danno happily nodded his head.

"Would you like to go inside?" Troy asked.

"I don't have time," Danno answered as he looked around for his wife. "I just need someplace safe to move some of my … " Danno lowered his voice, " … in case the government tries to fuck me over."

Troy nodded knowingly and held out a prepared file. "I've got the papers for your businesses here like you asked. I've placed Mrs. Garland ... "

"No," Danno simply said.

"Excuse me? I thought you were wanting to shift your assets into ... "

"I am. But not her." Danno felt his words betray his wife. "Not that I don't ... "

Danno's embarrassment caught his lawyer off guard.

"I'm just here to do as you say, Mr. Garland."

"We'll just think of someone else, that's all," Danno said as he hurriedly opened the file.

He didn't trust Annie with his business. He didn't know how the hearings were going to go. He didn't know if he was going to spend time inside or not. The last thing that felt right to Danno Garland was legally transferring everything he had to the woman he knew was running around behind his back.

"Who did he sign the business over to?" Katy asked.

Troy thought about how he was to answer. He wanted out of the cell in the worst way. He felt a certain loyalty to Danno over the years. But, here he was, cell number four and there was no knight on a white horse breaking down the door to rescue him. He always knew that the wrestling business was cut-throat. He just didn't think that he was far enough in to have to worry about it.

"Mr. Bartlett?" Katy asked again. "Who did Danno Garland sign his assets over to?"

CHAPTER SEVENTEEN

The First Precinct was small, too small for the amount of work that an under pressure city was throwing at it. Inside the front door stood the large booking desk, a fleet of filing cabinets, a couple of hand-marked doors and Captain Miller silently waiting by the restrooms.

His quiet demeanor made all the other cops working around him anxious. They pantomimed their work a little more to try and show him how hard they were trying. A couple of new officers even admonished a suspect in front of him and then dragged him away, thinking that's what Matthew Miller liked.

They were wrong.

He was only sitting there for one reason. And that reason walked in the door.

"You," he said to Nestor. "In here."

The captain stood and walked into the vacant interview room beside him. Nestor took off his coat and shook the rain off it. He watched as the other cops could hardly hold their delight at someone, anyone, getting called in to be yelled at.

Or, at least, that's what it looked like was going to happen.

Nestor thought for a fleeting second about walking past the open door and continuing on his way upstairs to his desk. He didn't have time for any of this bureaucratic bullshit.

But still he marched into the room like a kid going before a principal.

"Close the door," the captain ordered.

Nestor closed the door. Through the blind he could see the rapid exchange of information between his colleagues as to what they thought was happening.

"Sit down."

Nestor sat down.

"What happened with Danno Garland last night?" the captain asked.

"I don't know," Nestor answered.

"Two uniforms picked him up at the airport. They said that you were involved."

"Cooper?" Nestor asked.

Miller barely nodded in response.

Nestor seemed agitated that he even had to answer. "That asshole picked up Garland for nothing. If we're going to get something on him, we have to make sure that it's something that's going to stick."

"And what's that got to do with you, one way or the other?"

Nestor took a split second too long to answer. "Because of the conversation that you and I had in your office the other day. I wanted to see if there was anything to what you were saying. Help you out."

The captain slipped his hands in his pockets and rocked backwards and forwards on his heels. Nestor recognized this as Irish Cop Confidence 101.

"You were just helping your captain out?"

"Doing my job. Sir."

Miller saw a little too much attitude coming from Nestor.

"You're a liar," Captain Miller said bluntly.

"What?"

"You're lying to me. And I fucking won't have it."

"Are you accusing me of … ?"

"You're damn right I am," Miller said as he shot forward. "You're holding back on me about this man. You know things. You have a handle on what's going on out there with him and his crew. And you're still not telling me. And that leads me to think things I shouldn't be thinking."

"Not true."

"Not true?"

Nestor had enough. "Do you want me to talk honestly in here?"

The captain nodded again.

"There *is* corruption in this precinct – but not in this room."

The emergence of a silhouette through the blind stopped the captain's momentum. The figure outside knocked on the door. Neither man inside moved to answer it, so the waiting officer knocked again.

"Yeah?" Miller impatiently shouted.

A slightly nervous officer opened the door. "Sir?"

"What?" Miller walked around the table and right into the officer's face.

"Can't you get even a sense that I might be in the middle of something here?"

"Sorry sir, it's just … "

"What, it's just what?" Miller asked impatiently.

"Well sir … "

"What?"

"Central just told us that they got a call tipping them off about the location of a body Upstate."

"And?" the captain asked.

The officer had no choice but to respond in front of Nestor. "The tip-off said the body was put there by Danno Garland. Sir."

The captain was suddenly quiet. So was Nestor.

"Do you know anything about this?" Captain Miller asked Nestor.

Nestor shook his head.

"What do you want to do?" the officer at the door sheepishly asked.

There was no response. Only thinking. So the officer tried a little prodding. "If you think we have something on this guy, we should move now."

Nestor couldn't believe what he was hearing. How did this get by him? He knew Danno wasn't the killing kind. He figured it must have been something to do with the murder of his wife.

"This tip-off. Is it credible?" Nestor asked.

"Central say he left dates, times, places. It was someone who knew what they were talking about."

Nestor knew his boss was watching his reaction. He couldn't let it be seen that the new information affected him in any way.

"What do you want to do, sir?" the officer asked.

Captain Miller waited and weighed up everything he had before answering. There was no other answer he could give.

"Tell Central there is an ongoing investigation here and that we'll handle this."

Nestor jumped up from his seat.

"But not you," the captain said to Nestor. "You're staying here with me."

"And Danno Garland?" the officer asked.

"Find him. But hold the position. If there is something to this I want it done right. And above board. I don't want anyone doing anything without my say so."

Nestor tried to cover his disappointment and frustration. He did a bad job.

The officer left to relay the captain's orders.

"Enough of the bullshit. You're going to stay here and tell me everything you know about this man," the captain warned.

Ricky's heart thumped in his chest as he floored the pedal. He tore along the narrowing Seven Lakes Drive road. Either side of him were rust-colored trees and giant boulders stubbornly protruding from the ground.

Miles and miles of forest and trail. A perfect place to hide a body.

Unless someone rats you out.

Ricky wasn't even sure if Mickey Jack Crisp put the body where he said he was going to put the body.

But he had to find out.

There was Danno and his protection — Ricky always, always protected the boss — but there was also Ricky and his own protection.

As much as he hated being dragged in, he had the twisting stomach of a man who was clawing at the edge of a slippery black hole.

And he wanted to make sure he did everything he could to make it less slippery.

He thought of Ginny, alone. He thought of his life taken from him. All because of the actions of another man. He raged at himself for being so selfish. This business, *the* business came first.

He knew all the players were changeable.

In his rearview mirror Ricky saw a sight that stopped his breath. The impatient flicker of red and blue lights approaching him at speed through the thick Upstate fog. Otherwise, the road was empty and long. Had Tanner sold him out already?

He rushed through the contents of his car in his mind. Was there anything? Anything at all that they could pick up on? What about those tests he saw on TV that they can do now?

Ricky released his foot slightly from the gas and looked for any turning opportunity, left or right.

The siren grew louder and more intimidating as the green and black Plymouth Fury grew visible through the murk.

Quickly, they were upon him, aggressively pulling closer to his car and backing off.

What the fuck?

Ricky slowed down considerably and watched as the squad car overtook him and continued at full speed along the narrow road.

He slid to a relieved stop at the side of the road and watched his greatest fear melt into the distance ahead of him. Ricky had a quick laugh of pure relief.

Until it hit him.

They weren't looking for him. Yet. But they *were* heading where he was heading.

Ricky locked his steering wheel and screeched his car back towards the city. He couldn't do any more than he had already done about the body. Ricky knew the time was fast approaching for him and Ginny to run.

Danno felt he could breathe. In his own kitchen he felt a sense of natural sadness and remorse. He didn't know why, but he felt he could do that around Lenny Long.

With the side of his eye he watched his old driver dart around his cabinets and refrigerator.

"There's only eggs, boss," Lenny said.

Danno nodded and let Lenny continue. Lenny could see that there was obviously something wrong with Danno. He just didn't know how to ask. The timing seemed all wrong.

Danno liked that Lenny still called him boss. Those words made Danno feel something close to responsible for him. Like there was a bond between them. Maybe even a friendship.

When Lenny first came to Danno he was a 'mark'. He didn't know shit about how the business truly worked.

But now Danno saw him differently. He saw that Lenny had a goodness in him that was lacking in all corners of the business. Lenny *loved* wrestling. There were very few *in* the business who could say that.

Danno loved it once too. He was in awe of it when his father was boss. He was never allowed inside though. His father didn't seem to want Danno anywhere near wrestling. Now Danno could see why.

Lenny twirled the pan in his hand in a move of confidence. And dropped it on the floor. The clang of which nearly made Danno jump out the window with fright.

"What the fuck ... ?"

"Sorry."

Lenny picked up the pan, wiped it with his shirt and laid it gently on the stove.

It was getting overcast and cold outside. The open windows let some new life into the house, but with it came a cold nip.

"Can you take me somewhere, Lenny?"

"Drive you?"

"Yeah."

Lenny smiled. It had only been a little while but it felt like old times anyway. "It would be my pleasure."

"We'll have something when we get back."

Lenny definitely knew there was something really wrong. He never heard Danno turning down food before. "Okay."

Danno got up and leaned over to close the top of the window and saw a child wandering around outside.

There was a light tap on the door. "Dad?" Luke called from outside.

"Who the fuck is that?" Danno asked.

"It's my boy," Lenny said. "I told them both to wait outside."

Lenny opened the door and Luke was outside with his little brother in his arms. Both children looked scared and freezing.

"I played the song for him as long as I could in the car," Luke said to his father.

"Come in," Danno said to the young boys.

Luke waited for his father's okay before moving. Lenny motioned him into the house with a flick of his head.

"I just didn't want them making your house sticky," Lenny said to Danno.

"Not at all," Danno opened the door wider than Lenny had, and the two boys entered.

They were shaking, half from the cold and half from being left outside in the car as the night turned black. They weren't sure where their father was and they weren't sure when he was coming back. So Luke, seven years old, walked around the back of the house where he saw light.

"Does he stand?" Danno asked Luke of his little brother in his arms.

Luke was too scared to answer. He just gently placed his little brother standing beside him and helped his wobbly little body stand up straight.

"Answer the man," Lenny said to Luke.

"He … falls a lot but he's getting better," Luke shyly said to Danno.

Danno took a fifty out of his pocket and gave it to Luke.

"Are they coming with us?" Danno asked.

"I'm here without Bree. Just a flying visit."

"How about your mother?"

"She and my father are gone … " Lenny didn't want to bore Danno with the details. "She's not there either. We're just spending a night or two in her place and then heading back to Vegas."

"Vegas?"

Lenny nodded as they walked through the hallway.

"Where are we going?" Lenny asked.

Six days after the murder.

New York.

This was not a job executed with precision. There were several sets of tire marks that wore a perfect pathway, one deeper than the other, to the mound of freshly turned soil.

It was messy and the work of amateurs. The longer serving members of the department could hardly believe their luck. The tip-off was perfect in its placement of the body. The snitch brought them right to the mark and they were carefully treading all around it, so as not to fuck anything up.

"Precision," shouted one officer as they got out of their cars. "We do this one slowly and by the book."

They began to survey the area and more than one of the cops commented on it being a beautiful place to be buried. On the side of Bear Mountain, in a clearing of the forest and the fog, and with the Hudson in view - if you *had* to be executed and buried – this was the place.

A couple of uniforms cordoned off the area while another pair got suited up for the dig. By looking at the sloppiness of the site they were expecting it to be a shallow grave and a short day.

"Right, take it slow," came the order as the rain began to fall again.

With just the first shovelful of dirt they exposed a corner of black plastic. Just as it was described to them.

"Bingo."

"Already?"

"Yep."

Lenny took it easy in his father's two seat Ambassador. On the way to Danno's house he let the convertible top down to impress his boys and now he couldn't get it back in place.

Danno sat in the passenger seat with Luke sitting awkwardly on his lap. James Henry was on the floor of the car between Danno's feet, bawling loudly, tears streaming down his face.

"It's okay," Luke leaned down and whispered to his little brother.

"I think he shit himself," Danno said of James Henry.

Lenny opened the trunk and took out his travel bag and removed a diaper and a towel from it. He also checked to make sure the money he found in his hotel room was still at the bottom of the bag.

Lenny was just waiting for the right time to give Danno back his money and ask him for his wife's rings back. He couldn't wait to show Danno how loyal he was to him by returning all of the money that was missing from the rucksack.

He also couldn't wait to see Bree's eyes when she came back from her parents. Lenny regretted nothing more than taking his wife's rings and using them as collateral.

It was a worthless piece of shit move, and he knew it.

But the time just didn't feel right. Lenny could see that there was a major change in Danno since Lenny left New York. He just didn't know why. Because he was out of town, Lenny hadn't heard about Annie's death.

Danno and Lenny sat on the weather-worn bench at the foot of the cemetery. The two boys were charging around the grass in front of them, with bags of candy clasped in their hands. It was getting colder as the night wore on but sugar and horseplay staved off that reality for at least another while.

On the bench Lenny sat in shock as he listened to Danno talk about what had happened in Texas. Lenny had the bag containing Danno's money resting between his feet.

"They only found her the next day when she didn't answer her wakeup call. I went down there but they wouldn't let me take her. Said they needed to wait for someone to sign off on something. After all of our time together and I had to wait for someone else's permission to take her home."

"Why?" Lenny asked as he genuinely tried to think of a reason why anyone would harm such a lady.

Danno didn't hesitate to answer. "Because I tried to outthink everyone. I let her go to Texas. I let her get involved in this fucking business. And it … "

Danno took out the envelope Nestor gave him. "And that's what I have left."

Lenny wanted to do something or say something more substantial, but he had no idea how to fill the pause. What could he say? What could anyone say? He watched his former boss and idol wither before his eyes.

Listening to Danno's story of what happened to Annie reminded Lenny just how much he loved his own wife. And how much he missed her. He thought about how he'd love to stay but he just wanted to be wherever she was. New York, Nevada – it didn't matter.

Danno turned to Lenny with a crazed look in his eye. "Curt left me a message before … but I don't know what he meant," Danno said with utter confusion. "It wasn't light. The money was right, wasn't it?"

Danno could see his sudden intensity was making Lenny nervous. He stopped himself.

"Wasn't it, Lenny?" Danno asked calmly.

Lenny stuttered out a response. "What?"

"On the message, he said that the money was light."

Danno knew the rucksack came from Lenny's place. Lenny Long, he thought, the one person in the business who wouldn't fuck him over.

Lenny managed to muster up a slight shake of his head. "That's not true. The money was right."

If Danno had looked around he would have seen clearly that Lenny was lying. As all the pieces started to form in front of Lenny's face he could feel his stomach churn. The horror of what happened, and his place in it, began to make him feel dizzy and disorientated.

"Well then she was a stupid fucking bitch," Danno said out of nowhere.

Lenny nervously stood up and Danno immediately reined himself back in.

"The kids … I'm sorry," Danno said.

"No, no. It's cool," Lenny replied.

Lenny could see Danno pour over all the details in his head.

"I just don't know what the fuck happened," Danno said.

"I need to be out there," Nestor said.

"Why?" the captain asked. "What's your fascination with this man?"

The were both sitting now. The room was filled with Captain Miller's smoke. Nestor was now more openly anxious about what was happening outside the building. He didn't know what was going on.

"Why do you need to be out there?" Miller asked again.

"Do you have any idea how long I've been working for this

collar?"

"And still you let him go last night?"

"I need him outside. For now."

The captain laughed. "And why would that be?"

Nestor was too hot. He slid off his jacket and placed it on the back of his seat. It also gave him time to think. To try and say the right thing.

"Because he's making mistakes," Nestor said. "You know this is like a fucking equinox or something, captain, right? These men don't surface that often. And we have *the* boss running around out there with no one to rein him back in."

"What are you saying, detective?" Miller took another long pull from his cigarette and tapped the ash onto the floor.

Nestor knew that stonewalling was wasting his time. He needed to get going. He needed to get a position on Danno.

"I've been following Danno Garland on and off for a while," Nestor said.

"And?"

"And nothing. I have nothing. I was shaking the bushes to see what was going to fall out. That's all."

"And his lawyer? Troy Bartlett?"

Nestor paused a second. He didn't want to have to say any more. But he had to. "I have him. I've been shifting him around for the last few days."

Captain Miller nodded with a knowing smile. "Why?"

"Because I was trying to isolate Danno. Disorientate him. Anytime we pick up one of his guys for anything, this fucking guy, Bartlett swoops into the picture and has them released within a couple of hours. Danno isn't as strong without someone like him in his ear."

"Why all the running around?" the captain asked.

"Why?"

"Yeah, why?"

Nestor wondered just how much an old hand like Captain Miller could handle. How much truth he really wanted to hear. He decided to find out.

"Because I don't know you," Nestor began. "But we both know why you were placed here. We both know what the last guy in your position was. We know what most of the guys who work here are. Dirty. Dirty fucking cops."

"And you're not?"

Nestor shook his head and meant it. "I want to get this bastard. And I want to nail him on something that's going to stick. He has an office on West 42nd that's full of evidence that I'm fucking sure can pull them all down."

"Who are you getting that from?"

It was Nestor's turn to laugh. "His own fucking lawyer."

The desk officer knocked on the door again, only this time he didn't wait to be invited in.

"Sir, they've found the grave. Just like the tip-off said."

Nestor instinctively stood up.

"Sit," Miller said.

Nestor picked up his chair and slammed it legs first off the ground. He then sat down again like an angry, petulant child. He knew his case was being pulled from him and there was nothing he could do about it.

"They're waiting on your order, sir," the waiting officer said.

Miller was quiet in his seat. The order seemed straightforward, but nothing was forthcoming from the captain.

The cops on the scene were waiting for Captain Miller to swoop into the crime scene and get his picture taken and take the credit for the investigation. That's what all the other captains would do. But Miller wasn't moving.

"Sir?" the waiting officer said.

"Let *me* go and get Garland," Nestor pleaded.

Miller could feel the eyeballs on him. Waiting. Waiting for him to make the call.

"Captain?" Nestor asked again.

He had no choice.

"Tell them to proceed," Miller said.

The officer moved quickly away from the room.

Nestor was quietly livid. "He's going to pay his way out of this again."

Captain Miller flicked his cigarette at Nestor. "The only fucking one who looks dirty in all of this is you."

Danno apprehensively approached his wife's grave. He walked like a man who was sure she might in someway reject him.

He'd never been this close. When she was being buried Danno stood way back at the trees. He wasn't ready to say goodbye. Not without holding some form of apology. Not without some kind of justice for her.

He was taken aback by the starkness of witnessing his own wife's grave. It was too early to be anything other than a mound of dirt waiting for a headstone. But she was under there. He could see her in his head. Haunting him. Questioning him. Reaching out for him when she was on the floor and the last gasps of life were leaving her body.

Where was he?

Back in the cemetery parking lot, Lenny was in the car with his boys. Little James Henry was asleep in the dark on the passenger seat. He had Danno's coat over him and the tape of Bree singing playing softly in the background.

Luke sat on his father's lap and rested his head on his chest. He enjoyed the time alone with Lenny. It didn't happen often. Lenny was telling him a story with his lips but his mind was churning over the scenario that he was a part of.

"And then the giant walked across the ring and punched me right in the face. His hand was the size of a typewriter. And I went down like a ton of bricks in the cage."

A movement in the sideview mirror caught Lenny's attention. He noticed a cop flanking the car. And then another behind him. Lenny put his finger to his lips as he covered his son's mouth with his hand.

"Open," one cop whispered as he shone his flashlight through the window.

Lenny quickly rolled down his window. The cop studied the occupants of the car. Two children, and a man who looked nothing like the man they were looking for.

"Move along. Now," he said to Lenny.

"Okay," Lenny said as he quickly started his car. He counted ten more cops stooped over and walking carefully past his car. They all stopped at the gates of the cemetery.

At the crime scene, the rainwater was beginning to pool in various pockets of the plastic. Two white-suited officers were ready to expose the body just as soon as the photographer was ready and the word was given.

In the station, the captain and Nestor waited as the desk officer walked back and forth outside their open door with a large, grey, brick-like walkie-talkie in his hand.

"They're ready sir," the officer informed his captain. "We also have a team waiting to arrest Garland."

Captain Miller gave the tense, silent order with a nod of his head.

"I don't know what to do," Danno said at Annie's grave. "I want to follow you but I don't have the balls to do it. I want to kill the man who put you here but I can't. I fucking can't do anything to make this better and it's tearing me all up."

Danno finally began to mourn. His tears rolled down his face and his body began to shiver violently as he took in the reality of life without her.

Danno fell, one weak knee at a time, into the dirt and sobbed uncontrollably. "You've left me behind, Annie. There's nothing here for me anymore. I don't care about the money, or the business. I was just trying to show you that I'm a man. That I could get you everything that I thought a woman like you should have. I took over for you. I kept imagining you thinking of him. Comparing me and what I didn't have. I did your thinking for you. And it ended up poisoning me. The wondering and the guessing. I took over the business for you. So you'd love me more back. So you'd stop looking outside what we had to make yourself happy. I wish I talked to you more. I should have stepped in and told you, you were my wife and that I thought the world of you. I should have handled you better. And laughed with you more. I did you wrong when you were here with me. And I couldn't even make it right when you were gone. But I'm getting my due now. Here, on my own. I can understand you now. And it's too late."

Danno's tears turned to anger. "If I could make him feel something like this ... if I could just get my fucking hands on him."

Danno roared with frustration and fury.

"Are we ready?" called a voice from the crime scene grave site. "We have enough exposed to lift the plastic."

"Captain says go," shouted the officer on radio duty.

The freshly turned soil was now piled atop itself beside the newly excavated grave, and the black plastic sheet was exposed enough to lift it fully.

The photographer was shielded from the rain. "Ready," he said.

"Do it," the field detective said as he looked around to make sure everything was set.

The line of cops at the cemetery walls moved in quietly and quickly through the gate. They took up a new, covert position just inside the cemetery walls and waited for their next order.

"Well?" Captain Miller asked impatiently from the interview room.

"No word sir," the desk officer replied.

Just as the officer spoke, his walkie talkie crackled and a voice came through from the crime scene. "It's empty. Repeat, the hole is empty. There's nothing in there."

"It's empty?" Nestor asked. "Is that what they said?"

Miller stood. "Call them back. Do not approach Danno Garland."

Nestor smashed his chair against the wall. Miller stormed out of the office and cursed his way to his office upstairs.

CHAPTER EIGHTEEN

Ricky pulled up outside his apartment and quickly got out of his car. He was shaken, panicked and fumbling around with his keys. He didn't know what was happening or what Tanner Blackwell had told the cops.

"Ricky?" Nestor called as he crossed the street.

Ricky stopped suddenly, and instinctively contemplated running.

"You got a minute, man?" Nestor asked.

Ricky slowly turned. He looked around for other cops but didn't see anything out of the ordinary. He didn't even know if Nestor was a cop. But he had a strong feeling that he was.

"Can I come up?" Nestor asked as he came closer.

"Who are you?"

Nestor confirmed Ricky's suspicion about him by pulling out his badge and flashing it.

"And what do you want?" Ricky asked.

Nestor rested himself against Ricky's parked car. It was cold in the shadow of the building. Ricky didn't notice.

"Things are happening. Something is going down with all your people. There's things leaking out that are making my people very interested in you."

Ricky could hardly contain his body from shaking.

Nestor said quietly, "Before the day is out, they're going to get Danno. No doubt."

Nestor blew into his hands and rubbed them together. "All everyone downtown is wondering now is – who else is going down with him? How fucking big is that chain across the country? You know we'll get the evidence to find out."

Nestor could see that Ricky was doing a fine job in holding himself together. He needed to push more.

"How do you think Ginny is going to do with you on the inside?"

That was it. That was the perfect question to get Ricky to react.

"You ever threaten me again," Ricky said, "and I'll ... "

"Give up Danno. Come downtown with me. Then, when all this is over, you can move somewhere else and enjoy the last of your queer years on a farm or something."

"Are you here to arrest me?"

Nestor shook his head.

"Well then, why don't you get back to your job and find yourself a clean cop to shoot or something?"

Ricky opened his door.

"When I get Danno I know you're going to be coming in too. If you give him to me I can look after you ... "

Ricky slammed the door in Nestor's face. Nestor kicked Ricky's car in frustration.

"Fuck," he couldn't help but shout.

Eileen Dean felt bad. For most of her life she beat herself up about things she really shouldn't have. She was getting on in years and spent most of her time in Arizona with a man who came and went, which suited her perfectly. She wasn't close to her daughter who moved to New York about ten years before.

Eileen did what Eileen always did – she blamed herself. She was pretty much at home with the fact that she wasn't maternal. She just didn't have what she just didn't have. She fed and clothed her daughter and always made sure she was safe. Eileen just didn't do much in the way of affection.

And that ate her up too.

So in she flew to collect her grandkid. She wanted it to be different with him. She wanted to be the grandmother that she saw in her head. The one with the apron on, who was always tending to something delicious in the oven.

Eileen came into a little money when she sold her house, so now was the time. She invited her daughter and grandson to Disneyland. After all, that's where happy families went. At least in Eileen's head.

Eileen's daughter declined but Eileen was allowed take her grandson with her.

What a fucking mistake that was.

Eileen could hardly contain how much she hated him as they walked back to her car. She had just spent five days looking after the whiniest little prick she ever laid eyes on.

"That's too high, Nana."

"It's too hot."

"I've got a sore tummy."

"I miss my Momma."

"When are we going?"

"I don't like burgers."

"That mouse is scary."

He was fifteen years old.

Eileen was used to her own space. She thought she could manage. She couldn't. She was terrified that if he opened his mouth once more she might punch him in his tiny, spotty face.

She tried to spend her guilt away. And she was left to drag all that guilt with her through the massive parking lot. Half deflated balloons, toys, candy, hats, buttons and two huge suitcases.

She watched with disdain as her grandson walked with trepidation across the noisy parking lot. The only time he forgot where he was, was when he caught a glimpse of himself in a car window.

"Nana. Where is your car?"

"We're nearly there," she answered.

"Where is it, Nana?"

Even the way he called her 'Nana' she found weird and a little creepy.

"I don't know what it's called. It's beside the brown car straight ahead."

The grandson took off into a floppy run that was embarrassing to even look at. He came up to the back of Eileen's rental car and stubbed his sandaled toe, which propelled him face first into the trunk.

"Nana," he squealed.

Eileen used one of the bags to cover her face while she laughed as the image of him falling played over in her mind.

"Coming," she said between convulsions.

She tried to hurry with all her branded, plastic and sugared cargo. "Coming."

Eileen knelt down beside him. "Did you have an accident?"

"You saw it," he answered back.

"No, an *accident.*"

Eileen sniffed the air and her stomach turned at the smell wafting around.

"No," the grandson answered very matter-of-factly.

"Smells like you did," she said as she stood.

Then he began to smell it too. It was strong and pungent. And close. Eileen seemed to know instinctively that there was something wrong. The scent brought her to the brown Plymouth parked beside her. She cupped the windows and looked in.

"What is it Nana?" he asked.

She shushed him and continued her inspection of the car. His voice and they way her called her 'Nana' was making her stomach worse.

She noticed the car inside was messy in general and there was muck on the floor, but nothing to legislate for the type of stifling odor around them.

"It's coming from the trunk," he said, still sitting on the floor.

Ricky knew somewhere at the back of his head that it was going to end like this. Danno just wouldn't give up and that put them *all* at risk. The way the business was set up was - if anyone from outside the business got access - then it was only a matter of time before the whole business went down.

Their web-like setup was what made them so strong and, now that they were breached, it was that web-like setup that could put them all away.

Ricky Plick didn't have the time or the knowledge to hide what needed to be hidden. He wasn't familiar enough with the office to know what was legit and what should never be seen.

He just knew that somewhere in this office there was a lot of stuff that should never be seen by anyone outside the business.

And that's why he stood at the door of Danno's office on West Forty-Second with a canister of gas and a pocket full of matches.

He could feel the weight of his decision begin to settle down onto him. He walked the floor of the New York Booking Agency knowing that this office made Danno who he was. This room laid claim to the territories and the wrestlers. In their world, the contents of this office made Danno *the* boss.

Outside of their world, this office made them all criminals and thieves and match fixers. Outside of their world, the New York Booking Agency could end it all for everyone across the Americas.

And Ricky couldn't stand by and let that happen.

He chugged out the gas along the floor and dowsed the filing cabinets with it also. He threw it liberally left and right as he shimmied backwards towards the door.

He knew that the match he struck meant that they couldn't build a case against Danno based on his own records. He also knew this meant that if Danno couldn't lay claim to his territories and his champion, then *anyone* could.

With a strike of his match Ricky both saved and ruined Danno Garland.

He also threw the red meat of a vulnerable business to the men who wanted it all along. But what else could he do with the cops moving quickly in?

Ricky Plick, longtime right-hand man to both Danno and his father before him, threw the lit match and quickly closed the door to separate him from the quick and intense heat.

The only thing he brought with him was the contents of Danno's safe. He figured that would get him and Ginny out of the way for a while. Just 'til all of this settled down into whatever shape it was to take next.

The call came in and sent a concentrated pulse through Captain Miller. He couldn't stick to a fast walk. He burst into a sprint along the corridor.

"What the fuck is going on?" he shouted to no one in particular.

All the initial information pointed to it being Proctor King in the trunk of the brown Plymouth. The height, age and skin color matched. Danno was picked up in that same airport just the night before.

A few days prior, Ricky took five grand from Danno's safe. He didn't like that so many backstabbing snakes knew where all the evidence was. In an effort to clean up, Ricky personally threw Danno's gun in the Hudson and gave Mickey Jack Crisp the five grand to go back to Bear Mountain and move Proctor's body.

Mickey was halfway through this job when Danno contacted him to go to Texas.

But all Captain Miller knew was the snitch on the phone was good. The tip-off was reliable. They now had a serious case. They just needed Danno.

Miller just had to make sure one person didn't step in and fuck it all up - everything he built.

"Chapman. Get me Nestor Chapman," he shouted to anyone who passed him. "I don't want him anywhere near Danno Garland."

"He's not here sir," a passing officer replied.

CHAPTER NINETEEN

Five days after the murder.

New York.

There was a general sense of panic in Joe Lapine's hotel room. All the other bosses had gathered and they wanted answers from their chairman. There were threats thrown and new lines being drawn. There was finger pointing and jostling for position.

Joe was thinking, trying to make sense of the situation Danno had put them in. Tanner Blackwell was all out of thought.

"Enough," Tanner finally said as he rose out of his seat.

The room collectively calmed down and waited. It wasn't just the remaining bosses in the Americas present – it was the bosses from across the globe. They had arrived for Annie Garland's funeral and found themselves caught up in a meltdown.

"Danno Garland is going to be pulled today for the murder of Proctor King. I have it from someone on the inside," Tanner told the gathering.

Tanner's revelation sparked up the tension and confusion in the room again.

"Quiet."

Tanner was clearly delighted with what he had to say. "Now I know all of you are wondering what the fuck is going on and what's going to happen to us. But, this is the best of a fucked up situation folks. We got a boss, the one with the champion too, who kept pushing and pushing until something gave way. We all know that New York has been a mess since he took over. He's made his money and he could have passed the belt onto you or I like a gentleman. Instead he decides to do this and threaten all our livelihoods."

Tanner had the room by the balls. He was *feeling* it now.

"Now I heard you all talking about wanting to get the next plane out of here. Well, you go ahead and do that. I'm going to stay here and do what needs to be done. What my good Momma used to call 'pickin' the chicken'."

Tanner stopped his performance to light a cigar and take in the confusion of the room. They were all waiting on him now to make sense of a horrible situation.

"When Danno goes away, he's going to take all these problems we're having with him. But ... " Tanner paused. "He's also going to leave behind his treasure trove of goodies. He's got no one. It's not like he's leaving all his territories to anyone. Who has the fat fuck got?" Tanner asked with a laugh.

Joe had finally heard enough.

"Alright," he said from his sitting position. "It's time to retreat. There's no one in this room wants any part of this. Go back to your own territories and survive however you can until this all goes away."

Joe suddenly stood up and opened his hotel room door for them all to leave. "We need to go back to what we were."

Danno slipped on the cold arms of the suit that was lying on his bed. He was clean-shaven and wore his best shoes. He felt ready to move on. He noticed the reflection of the envelope that Nestor gave him sitting on the nightstand behind him.

His wife was gone, his business meant nothing to him anymore. He was old and had no one.

He took his waiting gun and jammed the barrel into his temple to see how far he would let himself go. His heart began to thump and his contorted face startled him. He began to fear just how easily the figure in the mirror was changing. No sleep, no wife, no revenge and no way to stop this choking pain. Danno sucked in angry breaths through his teeth and let them escape again, catching and projecting the saliva on his lips.

His body was petrified because his conscience held the gun. And Danno Garland's conscience was an angry, bitter and deluded place. It was gnawing at him, taunting him for being less than a man. For not being able to protect his wife and not even being able to avenge her death.

He peeled back the hammer and remembered instinctively the seconds before he killed Proctor in the clearing. It was the same. It felt the same. He felt the same.

His mind screamed at him that he was a fat, old fuck who was always going to be scared and less than a man. That he should have walked away and let Annie have the life that she wanted to live. Instead he stayed and forced her to be with him. How repulsed she must have been by him. How many times she must have laughed with Shane Montrose about him.

Danno moved the barrel from his temple to his mouth and clenched his teeth down hard. His trigger finger was paralyzed. He wanted something to remember her by.

He shook free the gun from his hand and walked over beside his bed. He rested on his knees and opened Nestor's envelope with a slice of his finger. He tilted it and an earring fell onto a crease in the bedclothes. Danno noticed it straight away and thought it might have been from a pair he bought her one year for her birthday.

He wished he could remember.

Remembering would have helped him believe that he was a better husband. That he noticed the little things and treasured his time with her.

He emptied the envelope totally and inside there were a couple of rings, a receipt and a wrapped, hard-boiled sweet that made Danno cry.

It was for her flight. To help pop her ears.

That he knew. That was his wife and something she would do. He couldn't contain himself as he remembered buying her the sweets and a magazine in the airport before she left.

And there was a scrap of paper.

Danno didn't recognize the rings, but that wasn't unusual. Annie had a little chest of jewelry that her mother left her when she died.

But the scrap of paper?

It read:

I'm sorry boss. I don't have all the money. I will pay you back. I promise. I'm sorry. Lenny.

Lenny?

Danno needed a second to think. To cobble together what was happening.

I don't have all the money? I will pay you back?

Danno wiped his eyes and slowly made his way to his feet, deep in thought.

Captain Miller stopped at the top of Danno's drive and scouted the huge house at the end of the drive. He could see no lights or signs of life, but decided to drive down slowly just in case.

"Wait here," he said to the two other patrol cars that were with him.

Inside the house Danno was turning over his kitchen with rage. He flipped his table and smashed the answering machine against his refrigerator. He then pulled his microwave onto the floor before twisting and yanking the open cupboard door off its hinges. He collapsed with his heart thumping too fast. He struggled to catch his breath. He felt himself snap. He could only bellow as he drove the back of his head into the sheetrock wall behind him. He knew Lenny had lied to him about the money being right. He thought Lenny had put his wife in peril. Lenny Long betrayed him. And his wife.

Danno would leave his house a different man. A vengeful man. A man who wanted Lenny Long to feel exactly like he felt.

Captain Miller parked his car and walked the steps to Danno's house. He looked back to see if the patrol cars had obeyed him. They had.

"Danno?" he shouted at the darkened house. "Danno, this is Captain Matthew Miller of the New York Police Department and I'm here to arrest you on suspicion of murder."

Miller banged the front door. "NYPD."

Danno crawled up the stairs and made his way to his room on his hands and knees. He was sucking in oxygen as he pulled the gun from his bed. He carefully peered out his window and saw a single car in the driveway. He then saw a figure walking to the back of his house.

Danno scurried and stumbled down the stairs and entered his kitchen carefully. The lights were on and it was obvious that he, or someone else, was inside. Captain Miller then appeared outside the kitchen window.

"You're obviously not here," Captain Miller said through the glass. "But if you were here, I would say to you that I was sorry to hear about Annie, Danno. You're not going to last another night on the outside. I'm sorry but I just thought you should hear it from me. Out of respect to your old man."

"Wait," Danno whispered through the glass. "I need to do one thing. I just need a little time."

Miller stood still, faced the door but said nothing. His silhouette was long and lean in the glass.

"There's money in the barn, third bale down from the door. On the right. Ten grand or more," Danno said.

Miller began to walk again. "You've got an hour."

Danno pushed out the cylinder on his gun and saw one bullet waiting.

It was the bullet that had Danno Garland's name on it from the start.

CHAPTER TWENTY

Nestor and Katy Spence sat silently in an unmarked car at the side of a darkened road. They both watched in silence as Captain Miller's car pulled out of Danno's driveway and was followed by two other patrol cars.

They noticed he had his radio to his mouth.

"What's going on?" Katy asked Nestor.

"Keep your head down," Nestor said as he crouched.

The cars were moving the opposite way but he didn't want to take any chances.

Nestor waited in silence until he was sure they were gone.

"What are we going to do now?" she asked.

"I'm going to drop you off somewhere. I appreciate the car but … "

He could tell she was not happy. Nestor leaned into Katy and kissed her gently.

"You've done great work on this case, Katy."

"I'm not going home. I want to know exactly what you're doing here."

Nestor took a second to ask himself how much he trusted this woman.

"There's something about the captain. I don't know, before you say anything. Just something."

He waited for a big reaction. A big rebuttal. There was none.

"Okay," Katy simply said. "What's your plan?"

Nestor turned on the ignition.

"I don't really have one," he said as he pulled slowly into the road. "I just want to finish this."

Nestor switched on his lights. They drove down the quiet road a little before noticing a car stopped on the side of the road.

As they drove past the car Katy's neck swiveled to the right. "Wasn't that … ?"

"What?"

Katy turned to look out the back window as Nestor drove. The parked car's passenger door closed.

"That was Danno Garland that got into that car."

"What?"

"Yeah. I'm sure it was him. He must have come out onto the road through the field next to his house."

"You sure?" Nestor asked.

"Yeah. One hundred per cent. He's in the car behind us."

Nestor looked back and saw the headlights of the car behind him appear around the bend.

"We need to pull in somewhere and get behind him."

In the car behind, Danno sat in the passenger seat. He didn't want to run the risk of taking a car of his own to Lenny's mother's house, so he flagged a car down.

The driver was a stranger, but a very well paid one.

Lenny watched his boys settle down on the couch. He knew he should probably go but they looked so comfortable. And Danno didn't know. Not that Lenny could tell anyways. He just didn't want to go back to Bree without her rings. Lenny gave them away and he wanted to get them back.

But he didn't know how to do that without telling Danno what happened.

Nestor and Katy kept their distance and followed Danno's car into a small, quiet, working-class street on Long Island.

"What are we doing?" Katy asked. "I thought Captain Miller told you all to contact him before … "

"I'm just looking."

Katy wasn't comfortable. "I think we should … "

"We're not doing anything wrong," Nestor reminded her as he pulled into a nice dark spot.

Danno's ride had done the same a few cars up.

Lenny saw car lights drift down his parent's street. Normally such a thing wouldn't even catch his attention, but this evening had him twitchy. Anxious even. He walked to the window and saw Danno getting out of a car he didn't recognize.

"Quick," Lenny said to his kids. "Up, up."

Luke sat up and rubbed his eyes. Lenny looked around for a quick, safe place. Just in case.

"Go and hide," he told Luke as he handed him his little brother.

"What's happening?" Luke asked.

Danno knocked on the door. "Lenny?"

His voice wasn't angry and his knock was light enough. But Lenny still wasn't sure.

"Go now," he said to his oldest son.

Luke got the message. He nervously ran for the kitchen pulling his brother along behind him.

"Don't make any noise," Lenny warned him. '

Danno knocked again. "Lenny."

Lenny made sure his sons were in the other room before he walked to the front door. He wasn't a religious man but Lenny said a little prayer before he opened the door.

Nestor and Katy watched Lenny let Danno into the house. It seemed calm and reasonable. Nestor was tossing around the politics of him being here without anyone else from his precinct.

"You're right," Nestor admitted. "It's not worth it."

"What?"

"Call it in."

Katy looked around for a payphone. She was willing to knock on doors and show her badge if she had to.

Danno closed the front door with his heel and produced his gun. He put it to Lenny's head.

"What are you doing?" Lenny was immediately paralyzed with fear.

The fright of seeing a gun and Danno's eyes go dead behind it made Lenny backpedal at speed. He put himself between Danno and his children.

"You fucking liar," Danno said. "You put her in harm's way."

"Wait," Lenny pleaded. "The kids. Wait."

In the kitchen Luke could hear the voice in the other room. He could see that his little brother was getting scared and agitated. He took him gently by the hand and led him out into the garage where he closed the door.

"We have to be quiet," Luke told James Henry as he put his finger to his lips. The dark was scaring the younger son. He began to cry and call for his *Dada*. Luke didn't know what to do.

"He can't come to you now, James Henry," Luke explained.

James Henry was tired and his gums were sore. He was in the dark and scared. He cried as he looked for a way out to find his father.

Luke looked up at his grandfather's car. "Come with me."

Katy got inside an old lady's house and made the call. Nestor sat in the car wondering whether or not his captain was dirty. It didn't feel right to him to stay seated when Danno was only a few hundred feet away from him. Nestor could finish his job and get the collar. He'd be known as the man who got the boss no one could get.

It was all right there.

Danno pushed Lenny back into a seated position and aimed the gun at his head. Tears rolled down his face as he saw his one-time driver in front of him.

"How could you do that to me, Lenny? How could you steal from me?"

"I ... "

"Can't you see what it did to me?"

"Yes boss. I didn't mean to ... "

"Shut up," Danno shouted.

Luke could hear the shouting getting louder in the house. His brother was sobbing on his lap in the passenger seat of the Ambassador. Luke wanted to make him better. Make him less scared. He moved his little brother, leaned over and turned on the ignition.

"Do you want to hear Mommy, James Henry?"

James Henry nodded.

Luke pressed play on the eight track and climbed back up into the passenger seat. As usual, Bree's voice coming through instantly settled the younger one. Even Luke got something from hearing his mother singing this time.

Both little boys sat in the dark, in a small garage, with the ignition running.

Danno left his gun on the table between him and Lenny.

"Take it," Danno said.

Lenny nodded.

"Take it or I will," Danno warned.

Lenny carefully picked up the gun.

"I'm sorry Danno," Lenny said. He meant it too. His heart was broken thinking of what happened to Annie.

"Use it," Danno said.

"What?"

"Shoot me."

Lenny moved to put the gun right back on the table.

"Lenny," he warned through gritted teeth. "There's one bullet and it's getting fired into one of our heads. That I promise you."

Danno couldn't take the pain of being alive anymore. "You will fucking know what I feel like."

"Danno ... "

Lenny was desperately trying to listen out for where his sons were.

Danno rose from his seat. He could now hear the sirens approaching. He could wait and spend his life in jail, or act and put an end to all of this.

"You have ten seconds to pull that trigger. You fucking hear me? You fucking cunt. You have ten fucking seconds to use that gun or I will. I want you to suffer through this for years. You hear me? I want your family to know that you killed someone. I want you to know what it feels like directly."

"I'm not going to do it."

"I have someone who will track down your wife, Lenny. He will spend every day of his life until he gets her. He's just waiting for the word."

The sirens were growing louder. Danno was growing more impatient. He was begging to be killed. To be reunited with Annie.

"If I leave here I will give him the word."

Lenny could see by Danno's eyes that he was serious.

"10 ... "

"I have the money," Lenny pleaded. "It was an accident."

Danno exploded with rage. "You think I want fucking money? I want you to suffer. I get no pleasure out of killing you Lenny. You hear me? You fucking understand me now?"

"But it was a mistake," Lenny said as he broke down. "It was… "

Danno grabbed Lenny by the collar and slapped him across the face. He pulled him out of his seat and locked him forehead to forehead. Danno's face was red and contorted with fury.

"Do it," Danno ordered.

Danno wasn't going to jail. There was no way.

"Do it."

Nestor knocked on the door. "Danno? Police."

Time was running out. The sirens had arrived outside and Nestor was now pounding on the door. Lenny was shaking with fear.

"I will find her. And kill her."

Danno threw Lenny back onto the seat and walked for his parent's phone.

"3 … " Danno counted.

Danno picked up the receiver and looked back.

"2 … "

Lenny stood. "Don't."

"Danno," Nestor shouted once more before he kicked the door.

"1 … "

Lenny fired a single shot at Danno's head that killed him instantly. Danno's body fell to the floor as Lenny dropped the gun. Nestor broke through the door and fired a round that hit Lenny in the chest. The impact lifted him back into the seat. He was alive but choking on his own blood.

"Medic," Nestor shouted as he entered the house with his gun still raised. "We need a medic."

Lenny tried desperately to tell him about his kids but he couldn't speak through the blood that was filling up his mouth.

Nestor kneeled down beside Lenny. He recognized his face from his investigation.

"Lenny?" Nestor asked.

Lenny tried to talk but he was choking.

Five hours before Danno's murder.

Katy Spence was listening intently to Danno's lawyer. She still didn't feel like he was going the whole way. She needed to know exact details.

"Who did he sign the business over to?" Katy asked.

Troy thought about how he was to answer. He wanted out of the cell in the worst way. He felt a certain loyalty to Danno over the years. But here he was, cell number four, and there was no white knight breaking down the door to rescue him. He always knew that the wrestling business was cut-throat. He just didn't think that he was far enough in to have to worry about it.

"Mr. Bartlett?" Katy asked again. "Who did Danno Garland sign his assets over to?"

Troy could see the file in his mind. He took it from the barn where Danno signed it and placed it deep into his own filing cabinet.

Katy tapped the cage to get his attention.

Troy's head shook in amazement at what he was about to say. "He didn't trust his wife for some reason."

"Who did Danno Garland sign his business over to?" Katy asked more pointedly.

Troy looked her dead in the eye. "His driver."

The End.

LINKS AND INFO

NOTIFY

I truly hope you enjoyed Vol. 2. If you would like to sign up to be contacted when Blood Red Turns Dollar Green Vol. 3 is available, please visit:

http://www.paulobrien.info/notify

It's a one step process that only takes a couple of seconds.

FREE STUFF!

Also, if you review Blood Red Turns Dollar Green Vol. 2 on Amazon, I will send you a free, signed, Special Edition Duology of Blood Red Turns Dollar Green and Blood Red Turns Dollar Green Vol. 2 free!

http://www.paulobrien.info/free

The amount of stars you give, of course, is completely up to you.

WEBSITE

And finally, my website is always up-to-date with the latest news, blogs, competitions, reviews and much more:

http://www.paulobrien.info

Thank you for reading Blood Red Turns Dollar Green Vol. 2. I hope to see you again soon for the last installment of this series.

We're headed for the 80's baby!

ABOUT THE AUTHOR

Paul O'Brien is a writer from Wexford, Ireland. In the last fifteen years he has written sixteen plays and two screenplays. He has been commissioned or produced by The Abbey, Druid, Red Kettle Theatre Company, Town Hall Theatre, Galway and Spare Key Productions in New York.

Blood Red Turns Dollar Green, his debut novel, became a #1 Bestseller in both the US and UK in 2013.

Printed in Great Britain
by Amazon.co.uk, Ltd.,
Marston Gate.